He sat in a large chair, thinking and muttering aloud,

contemplating what he wanted to do, what he needed to do, with Kate McCoy. He thought of her unmistakable face, of her beauty. Then he thought of Kaitlan McGregor.

And the two of them blended into one.

He thought of the rich, full mouth they shared, and he longed to kiss it. He thought of the soft, tawny hair, and his fists clenched, his fingers wrapping tightly around the arms of the chair. Oh, how he wanted to run his hands through that softness, move his fingers down to her slender throat.

Where he wanted to slowly squeeze the life out of her once and for all.

He'd killed her before, of course. Three times, as a matter of fact.

This time, he'd make sure he did it right.

Dear Reader,

We've really got a special treat for you this month—two brand-new authors whose way with dark romance spurred us to create "New for November" this month, only in Shadows.

First up is Cheryl Emerson with *Treacherous Beauties,* the tale of a woman drawn to the isolated town where her brother met his untimely death. There she is forced to confront not only her brother's specter but also the possibility that she might be falling in love with a wealthy, handsome man—who just happens to be a murderer!

Time itself plays tricks in Allie Harrison's *Dream a Deadly Dream.* Kate McCoy's dream lover was so perfect. If only he could be real. And he was! A flesh-and-blood man driven to travel through the night to make love to a stranger, an experience they both recalled as a dream until forced to accept it as reality. But why was fate so determined to bring them together? And what was their connection to a string of murders spanning a past neither could have known?

You'll be thrilled and chilled by this month's selections, but be sure to come back next month for more of the eerie passion you can always find here on the dark side of love, here in the Shadows.

Yours,

Leslie Wainger
Senior Editor and Editorial Coordinator

ALLIE HARRISON

Published by Silhouette Books
America's Publisher of Contemporary Romance

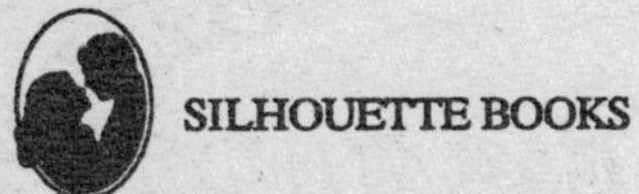

ISBN 0-373-27020-8

DREAM A DEADLY DREAM

This edition published by arrangement with Harlequin Enterprises B. V.

Printed in U.S.A.

ALLIE HARRISON

has been writing since she was in school, but never really took it seriously until she joined her local RWA chapter three years ago. She now works to divide her time between her husband, their two small children, reading the latest hot romance and creating her own intriguing stories.

She lives in a small town in Southern Illinois and believes people should follow their dreams and never give up.

To Wayne, Ben and Rachel,
and to my parents, Doc and Virginia,
for all your love and support

CHAPTER ONE

Warmth pressed against her lips, spread through her body.

Kaitlan relaxed against the sensations flowing through her and no longer fought to bring herself awake. Why wake up when a dream could be so real?

"Kaitlan."

Kaitlan had never believed that the whispered sound of her name could cause her flesh to tingle and a shiver to move up her spine. But it was like a soft caress to her ears, moving through her body all the way to her soul.

She sighed, feeling the warmth of his lips move down her throat. They suckled gently at her pulse, causing it to quicken with the racing of her heart. A warm hand cupped her breast, and Kaitlan's breath caught in her throat. Then his lips found their way to the same spot. He took her breast in his mouth and teased her nipple with his tongue.

Kaitlan groaned and nearly came right up off the bed, feeling as though a bolt of lightning had struck her somewhere in the pit of her stomach. Her total being cried out, her flesh feeling alive and on fire.

His mouth remained as his hands moved down to explore the rest of her body, touching her, tickling her near her hipbone. Then his lips crossed an imaginary bridge to her other breast and cast the same assault.

Kaitlan was panting, trying to draw in oxygen, even though the need for oxygen no longer seemed important. What he was doing to her was the only thing that mattered. His fingers on the inside of her thighs were more than she could bear. She knew she would die without his touch.

"Please," she whispered. "Please."

"You want me?" he asked, his voice nothing more than a hard whisper that seemed to come from inside her own mind.

"Yes." She forced out thc word. She could barely speak, her throat was so tight. Her entire body was tight.

He touched her with one finger, and Kaitlan cried out. He laughed softly at her response. "Say you love me," he ordered.

"I love you," she said. At that point, she would have said anything, would have done anything.

He moved over her, settling so close that Kaitlan could feel his breath on her face. She forced her eyes open and could see only the dark form of his face above her. Yet she knew exactly what he looked like; she knew every distinct feature and line of his face. She knew his hair was light brown and his eyes were dark.

His lips returned to hers in a hot caress that threatened to reach her very soul. Oh, what a dream! He moved between her thighs and took possession of her body in the same soul-searching way, filling her as though he had been made just for her.

She held on to him, pulling his body against her as hard as she could, feeling the muscled softness of his back with her hands.

"Say it again," he said.

"I love you." Her voice was harsh, her throat dry.

Then it was as though he did, indeed, reach to touch her soul. He reached again and again until he finally touched it in a way that caused her to cry out again, and it left her panting and exhausted.

"Oh, Jacob," she breathed. She'd known his name. And she wondered only briefly how she could have known.

"Yes, love?"

"It never felt like that before."

"For me, too," he whispered in her ear, his breath warm and familiar.

She felt him move away from her. "Don't leave me," she said.

He rolled over next to her and pulled her into the warmth of his arms, arms that felt massive and strong.

"I can only stay a while, Kaitlan," he whispered. "But I'll leave you a rose to show you my love." The front of him was pressed against the back of her.

Kaitlan smiled in her sleep. She could feel every curve of him, every contour with distinctive detail. "What a dream," she muttered, letting the dark realms of sleep take her away again into nothingness.

"It was no dream," she heard his voice loud from somewhere within her own sleeping world.

"Of course it was. I don't know anyone named Jacob."

"You've known me forever," he replied.

It wasn't important. Now only sleep was important. She snuggled against him and fell fast asleep.

Some time later, she felt him move off the bed and leave her. She rolled over and forced her eyes open long enough to glance at the clock on the bedside table. It was 5:03, much too early to get up. She let sleep take her once again.

* * *

The morning light in her eyes woke her. She rolled over to look at her clock on the bedside table. Seven-thirty-four.

Kate McCoy jumped out of bed. She was usually on her way to the school by this time. There was no time for her shower. She took two steps toward the bathroom and stopped. Her body was sore, she felt as if she'd run a race all night. And her night gown was gone!

She looked down at her naked body as though she'd never seen herself before. She turned and looked back at the bed. Her white cotton gown was in a heap on the floor.

Then the dream flooded her memory, filling her thoughts completely. His face flashed through her mind. She remembered every single aspect about him. How he looked, how he smelled, the feel of his muscular, soft skin, the taste of his kiss. She remembered every touch. She remembered the way her body responded to those touches. She stood planted for a moment, unable to stop the warmth that spread through her again.

"What a dream," she muttered, running her hand through her hair. It had been some dream, wild enough that she'd removed her own nightgown in her sleep. Her body came to life again just thinking about it. She had to put the memory out of her mind. She had to. She had small children to teach.

She trod into the bathroom. The reflection that stared back at her from the mirror looked wild. The short tawny waves of her hair were going in every direction, her cheeks were flushed and rosy, there were faint, dark circles beneath her eyes. Of all days to look like this. Oh, she needed a shower. And there simply wasn't time.

She brushed her teeth and put on her makeup quicker than the speed of light. She brushed her hair, pulling it hard. But she had the feeling it didn't matter how hard she brushed. It seemed to have a mind of its own today. And short of washing it, nothing was going to entice it to lie as she wanted it. Her waves were going to spend the day standing out in all directions, looking as if she'd spent the night in a wind tunnel. She sighed heavily, looking at herself. She felt as if she'd spent the night in a wind tunnel. She turned back and headed to her closet where she dressed just as quickly in the brightest red blouse she owned. Something bright to keep her awake.

Kate walked to school, even though she was late and the clouds threatened rain. The fresh air gave her much-needed energy. But the time alone allowed her thoughts to drift back to her dream. She again had to force them away to concentrate on the day's lesson plan. She managed to arrive at her classroom four minutes before the bell rang. This was not a good way to start the day, she thought. She always liked to have at least fifteen minutes to settle herself before she was forced to deal with seventeen six-year-olds. Normally, if she had to rush in the morning, the rest of the day was a rush as well.

Today was no exception to that rule.

The children were just as unruly as she didn't need them to be, always at the point of trying her patience. Little Marion White spilled her milk at snack time. John Gill broke the lead of his pencil and sharpened it until there was very little of it left. To top things off, it started to rain just before recess, and Kate was forced to keep them all inside to play.

Janey Martin and Gwen Paulsonn fought over a doll and managed to tear the head off it before Kate could intervene. Then at rest period, when they were all supposed to be lying on their mats, listening to the storytime cassette while Kate took her own break at her desk, Tommy Castle came up to ask if he could go to the washroom. Then he bumped her cup, spilling nearly an entire cup of coffee all over her desk blotter and lesson planner.

Throughout all of this, her dream continued to flash through her mind. It was frustrating the way the memory kept recurring, bringing heat to her flesh and refusing to leave her until she forced it away.

By the end of the day, Kate was ready to pull out her hair, and she was glad to see the children go. But after they had gone, she found herself wishing they hadn't. For then she was left alone again with her thoughts, left alone with a dream that still seemed so real.

"You look like you've had a rough day," said Maddie Jackson, who stood leaning against the doorframe. "If you can't handle first grade, we'll have to send you back to kindergarten."

Kate smiled, glad to see her friend. "Now you're going to tell me that your fourth-graders were a breeze today, too, I guess."

"Of course they were," Maddie replied. "They always are on Fridays."

Kate was packing papers to check and her wet, sticky lesson-plan book into her bag.

"Do you want to meet Gabe and me at the Main Line for some supper? They're having the all-you-can-eat fish special tonight." Maddie shifted her position and leaned against the other side of the frame.

"No, thanks," Kate replied. "I need some rest."

Maddie smiled easily. It was what had drawn Kate to her when she had first arrived in Port James the year before to teach. "Were you up all night again watching those old movies on your VCR?"

Kate picked up her bag and turned to her friend. "No," she said seriously. "Maddie, have you ever had a dream that was so real, you were tired the next morning?"

Maddie didn't reply right away. "No," she said finally. "Not that I can remember. I've had dreams where I keep waking up between them, and then I'm tired. But I don't remember ever being tired from an actual dream. Why?"

"Because I had one," Kate said simply. "My body's even sore. I feel like I worked out for two hours."

"Did you run a marathon?"

"No." Kate paused, feeling herself flush. "It was . . . erotic."

Maddie grinned. "Oh, one of those."

"What do you mean 'one of those'?"

"I think it's time you went out on a date, that's what I mean," Maddie shot back, still grinning.

"A date?"

"Yes, a date. You remember, one of those things where you spend some time with a person of the opposite sex. You go out, maybe have a nice dinner, some polite conversation, and then you get kissed on your front porch when it's over." Maddie was still grinning. "Unless, of course, you don't want it to end. In which case, you invite him in for dessert."

Kate looked at Maddie. She already felt drained from what must have been a nearly sleepless night. Maddie's words could have been spoken in a different language for all the effect they had on Kate. She was just too tired. And—she was not ready. Not yet. The thought of dessert, even dinner or anything else with a man made Kate want to turn and walk in the opposite direction. Maybe even run. Because her fear was still just a little stronger than her loneliness.

Still, she knew Maddie wanted only the best for her. So for now, she humored her. "And just who do I choose for this spectacular event?"

Maddie's brows rose, since she knew no real answer to the question.

"You know," Kate went on, "the only decent man left around here was Gabe, and you took him. Now all that's left are men who are old enough to be my grandfather and men who smell like fish. And in most cases, those two qualities are combined."

Maddie bubbled with laughter. "You don't make this easy."

"It's not easy," replied Kate, her face growing serious.

Maddie grew serious, too. "You know I just worry about you. You're my friend, and I hate to see you hurting. How long has it been since you signed the final papers?"

"I'm not hurting anymore," Kate replied, avoiding the actual question. "I'm just being cautious."

Maddie refused to let it die. "It's been nearly a year since your divorce, hasn't it? And how many months before that did he move out and move in with that—"

"Please, Maddie, I don't want to talk about it." Kate turned away, pretending to look for something on her desk. Yet no matter how hard she tried to turn away from it, the hurt was still there. Not the hurt in her heart. That hadn't lasted long at all. It was the hurt to her pride. Her wounded pride that continued to remind her that her husband—ex-husband—dumped her for one of the young, spring-chicken students of the college class he taught.

"I'm sorry." Maddie stepped into the room and closer to Kate. "But I can't let you stand here and continue to let him hurt you. He took so much from you already. Don't let him take the rest of your life, too. Besides," she was back to her grin "—not all men are alike. And they don't all smell like fish, you know."

Kate chuckled, feeling lightened with the turn in the conversation. "You're right."

Maddie placed a companionable arm about Kate. "I know I'm right. I dated a few of them myself, before I caught Gabe."

"How did we even get on this subject?" Kate asked. "I was telling you about my dream." She paused. "It was so real," she said slowly.

"So what did he look like?"

"Who?"

Maddie rolled her eyes. "The guy in your dream, who else?"

"It was the strangest thing. I couldn't see him, it was too dark. But somehow I know his hair was light brown, like it was touched with gold, and his eyes were dark. And he made me feel like he could see right into my soul when he looked at me."

Maddie's brows raised. "I think you may have missed your calling. You should be writing poetry or something."

Kate sighed heavily, knowing it was no use. How could she explain something she didn't even understand? She quickly changed the subject. "What time are you meeting Gabe?"

Maddie glanced up at the clock on the wall. "In about ten minutes."

"Then you'd better go, or you'll be late."

"Can I give you a ride home first?" Maddie asked. "It looks like it could rain again."

Kate shook her head. "I have my umbrella, and I'd rather walk."

"All right," Maddie replied, her voice full of reluctance. "Listen, if you're not planning anything tomorrow, why don't you give me call. We could hit some antique shops or something. Who knows, maybe we could get lucky and find some great bargains to help fill up that big house of yours."

Kate nodded, slinging her bag over her arm. "That sounds great."

They walked to the door together.

"See you later." It was evident Maddie didn't want to leave her.

But Kate didn't want her to worry. "I'll call you later."

They finally parted, and Kate was glad to be alone. She was glad to be on her way home, to get outside where she took a deep breath of salty, moist air. For some unknown reason she felt as though telling Maddie about her dream had been a mistake.

For the first time all day, she actually allowed her thoughts to dwell on the dream. She remembered it with as much detail as though a movie were playing in her head. She thought of each touch. She thought of the way his skin felt to her. She thought of the sound of his voice. Perhaps Maddie was right. Perhaps Kate did need a man, or least a date. She had been in Port James for months and had yet to see a man who even sparked her interest.

She absently watched a car pass. Hadn't that car passed her before on the last block? Perhaps. Kate didn't dwell on it; she was still thinking about the dream.

She turned the corner and moved into the last block before reaching her house. She was proud of her big, Victorian house. It was the first place she actually had felt welcome and at home. And it was all hers. From where she was standing, she could see the point of its towered roof.

A little farther up the walk, Kate stopped. Now she could see the wide porch in the front and most of the driveway. The car she thought had passed her twice sat parked behind her car, and she could see a man waiting on her porch.

She walked on again, never taking her eyes off him. His back was to her. It was his hair that held her. His hair, the color of brown, touched with gold. Even on a cloudy day like this, with no sunlight to touch it, his hair was still reflecting gold.

She made it to the end of her walk and silently climbed the steps up to the porch. He turned, knowing she was there. His gaze met hers and held, his brown eyes holding an expression of surprise and expectation at the same time. Kate remembered that look. His eyes had held that same look just before he started to make love to her, just before he slipped inside. . . .

Kate nearly had to shake her head to clear it and stop the film of memory that wanted to play over again and again.

Seeing him standing before her was enough to cause her heart to flutter and stop the flood of memories. It was he. It was the man in her dream! Kate couldn't believe she was actually standing face-to-face with him, looking at him.

They stared at each other for a long moment that could have been mere seconds or several hours. Kate had no idea. She had the sudden desire to turn and run. Yet at the same time, she wanted to fall into his arms and feel his familiar touch. She had never felt so torn in two different directions in her life. In the end, she did neither, for her legs simply refused to move.

She tore her gaze from his to finally look down at what he held in his hands. A pink rose. A single pink rose.

Kate's knees grew weak at the sight of it. "I'll leave you a rose to show you my love," she muttered, unaware that she'd actually spoken. She stared at it with wide eyes for a long moment while she worked to catch her breath. Then her gaze moved up to once again meet his.

His brows rose at her words, and she nearly gasped. She remembered his eyes had looked just like that, all filled with dark brown smoke, just before he kissed her in the dream. If he kissed her now, she knew her knees would give out beneath her.

He didn't kiss her, though.

Instead, he spoke one word. The one word that had nearly the same impact as a kiss would have. It sent a shiver up her spine and caused her flesh to tingle with a life all its own again. "Kaitlan."

CHAPTER TWO

"Who are you?" she asked, her voice feeling tight. The dream washed through her mind again with a sudden intensity that frightened her. She remembered how his lovemaking in the dream had made her throat tight, just as it was now.

"Jake," he replied, his voice sounding harsher than before. Perhaps his throat was tight as well, she thought. "Jake Casperson."

Kate's brows knit. "I called you Jacob last night," she noted.

He ignored her comment. "And you're Kaitlan."

Kate shook her head in disbelief. "Just Kate. Kate McCoy."

He stared down at her for a long moment, and the look in his eyes caused more than just fear to shiver up her spine. "How the hell did you do that?" he questioned, his voice growing with anger.

"Do what?" She looked up at him with wide eyes.

"Get into my dream," he replied evenly. His eyes grew even darker, more intense. "And you're talking about it like it really happened."

Kate slowly shook her head. She knew she should get far away from him as fast as she could, but her feet still refused to move. Kiss or no kiss, her knees had little more substance than water. "I didn't do anything. It was my dream. It was my bed," she replied defensively. She clamped her mouth shut suddenly. God, what was she saying? Her insides were quivering as though she might break apart at any second. And her body, her mouth included, was taking no instructions from her brain.

"A warm bed with a patchwork comforter," he said simply.

Kate had no idea what to say. She slowly nodded.

It was like déjà vu. Kate had been with him. She knew him, knew how he smelled. She remembered the taste of his kiss, the sound of his voice, the feel of his heart racing in unison with hers. And she remembered the way he felt inside her, so perfect, so right.

And yet, she didn't know him at all. She'd never seen him before. At least before the dream. Or had she? She suddenly wasn't sure.

Thunder clapped in the distance, and the first drops of rain began to hit the roof of the porch with small pitter-patter sounds. Kate was vaguely aware of it. She still found it impossible to take her eyes from the man before her.

"Was it witchcraft?" he asked, his question breaking her silent study of him.

"What?" she stammered.

"Witchcraft," he replied, his voice growing firm. "I never really believed in any of that stuff before today."

Kate shook her head again. "I told you, I didn't do anything."

"Well, I sure did," he snapped. "I drove around for nearly an entire day looking for this house, looking for you. I don't even know why. I kept telling myself you couldn't possibly exist, that you were just a figment of my imagination."

Kate's brows rose in surprise and she blinked several times at his words. Surely, he could see she was more than just a figment of any imagination—even his. "Are you telling me you drove around aimlessly for hours looking for me?"

"At first, I did," he replied speculatively. "Until I remembered something you said when you greeted me last night."

"Oh?" She didn't remember greeting him at all, and she was afraid to ask. "And just what did I say?"

He never took his eyes from hers. "You said, 'It's about time you made a trip back to Port James, stranger.'"

"I never said that," she muttered. Yet there was no denying that the words were vaguely familiar. "Mr. Casperson—"

He cut her off. "So here I was in Port James, looking for your house, feeling like something was leading me to you. Then I saw this tower." He paused to glance at the round corner on the other side of the porch. "And I knew it was yours. Just what the hell happened last night?" he demanded, exasperated.

"I don't know."

She stopped, took a deep breath and mentally counted to ten. Teaching first-graders gave her a lot of practice doing that. "Mr.Casperson—" she started again.

"Jake," he put in. "I don't know about you, Kaitlan, but I feel we deserve to be on a first-name basis after last night."

"It's just Kate, I told you," she said softly, trying to keep some control in her voice.

"Oh, yes," he said, his lips twisted into a tight-lipped grin. "Kate McCoy." Kate didn't like the way her name seemed to roll off his tongue, touched with a bit of sarcasm. This was not her fault. She had no control over her dreams. Did she?

There was an uncomfortable moment of silence between them.

"Why don't you come in," she offered. "We can talk about this over a cup of coffee. Maybe if we talk about it, we can get past it and move on with our lives."

Jake looked at her hard, as though he didn't believe that was possible. "Cappuccino?"

"Of course, but I'm afraid it's instant," she replied automatically. She stopped suddenly, feeling violated that he even knew what kind of coffee she kept in her pantry.

She pulled out her keys and unlocked the front door, her hands shaking. Jake followed her into the house, not really looking about as any other newcomer might. There was an air of familiarity about him, as though he'd really been there before. As though he didn't need to look at her array of antiques—he'd already seen them before. He followed her past the stairs into the kitchen without any hesitation. He even sat down at her kitchen table in the chair opposite the one where she always sat. She went about making coffee without looking at him.

"Tell me what you dreamed," she said.

She turned slightly to see him place the pink rose on the table in front of him.

"I dreamed of you. I dreamed of this place," he replied simply. "The entire town is familiar, even though I don't remember much of it being in the dream."

His voice was now as she remembered, and the huskiness of it caused her to pause in reaching for two cups. Her hands were still shaking slightly. "And just what did you dream of me?" she asked slowly.

"I dreamed I made love with you," he replied evenly. His words were simply spoken and right to the point. He could have been telling her the sky was blue.

Kate turned to meet his eyes and found his cheeks were spotted with color. She breathed deeply again and poured the coffee. Then she brought the cups to the table and set one before him.

She took a sip, letting the hot liquid warm her mouth and wash away the cold feeling she had, which came from more than just the damp, cold weather. "I dreamed of you, too," she said slowly.

"That we were in bed, in your bed?" He took a sip as well. A big sip, Kate noticed. Maybe he was feeling just as cold inside. She fought the urge to reach out and take his hand. Why would she want to hold his hand? She hardly knew him. Yet, looking at him, she did feel as though she knew him, had known him for a long time.

Kate nodded and met his eyes again. She could find no words to describe his expression. He was looking at her with something close to desire, and Kate found herself remembering the feel of his lips and wishing she could feel them again now. She took another swallow of coffee. Anything to give her mouth something else to think about.

"Unbutton your blouse," he ordered.

Kate nearly choked on her coffee. "What?"

"I want to see your birthmark."

Her hand instinctively moved to the place just below her left collarbone where she had a small strawberry mark.

He no longer needed for her to unbutton her blouse; her movement was enough to confirm his suspicions. "It's there, that mark that looks a little like a question mark," he stated.

"Yes, it's there." She attempted a small laugh. "This is all quite ridiculous, you know. I mean it was just a dream. You weren't really here. You couldn't have been."

"There's more than two hundred extra miles on the odometer of my car that says I went somewhere," Jake put in.

"But all my doors were still locked from the inside this morning."

It was so hard to believe, it was frightening. But still, Kate couldn't seem to turn away or ignore any of it. In fact, what she was feeling wasn't exactly fright. She was remembering the way he'd made love to her, the way her body responded to his every touch.

"You let me in," he said, looking directly at her in a familiar way.

"I did?" She felt like laughing again, but didn't.

"Yes. I knocked on the glass of your back door," he stated simply, his eyes shifting to the back door behind her. "And you let me in."

"That's impossible." Something rippled through her, but Kate wasn't quite sure what it was. A memory? Fear? Horror? Panic? Dread? Or was it lust? She couldn't deny the fact that she wanted his arms around her. His strong arms that made her feel so safe. She didn't want to feel safe with him. She knew she shouldn't feel safe at all. She could tell by looking at him that he was dangerous, a man she didn't need in her life. The air in the room was suddenly hard to breath. "Perhaps you should go," she said softly. She needed to be away from him before she did unbutton her blouse.

"Not yet."

"Why not?" She tried to look at him evenly, so he couldn't know how out of control she felt. "It's over. It's done with. Even if, and I mean if, it was more than just a dream last night, then there's nothing we can do to change what's already happened."

He set his cup down with a small thud. "It's not over."

Kate felt a warm flush move up her neck to her face. His eyes left hers, seeing it. His satisfaction was evident in his features. "See, I told you it wasn't over. Whatever it is that brought us together is still here." He paused, taking a sip of coffee. "And it wants us to be together."

"That's absurd," she spit. "It's more than absurd. It's crazy!" Did he expect her to simply take off her clothes and jump into her bed with him because he thought *something* wanted them to be together? Kate laughed this time.

"Is it?" he asked calmly. "What are you feeling, Kate?" He was looking at her, his eyes telling her he already knew exactly what she was feeling. "Fear? Or desire? Are you worried about what exactly brought me here to you? Or are you just wishing I would kiss you?"

Dear God, was he reading her mind? "This is crazy," she said again, this time with more emphasis, hoping to get through to him.

"Oh, yes." He grinned. "I kept thinking it was crazy the whole time I was driving here. I kept thinking that I was crazy. I had to be. But still, I couldn't stop until I found you. Not until I found out for certain that you had white kitchen cabinets with glass panes. Or that you had a pencil-post bed with white sheers on the posts and a patchwork quilt that your mother made for the comforter. Or that your living room was wall-papered with small violets in a vertical pattern."

Kate's eyes widened with each instance. "Oh, God," she whispered softly. The horror of his words were sinking in, overriding whatever desire she'd felt before. The fact that he knew in great detail such small aspects of her life was more than horrifying, it was amazing, truly amazing. She didn't want to know this. She wanted to go back to her job and live her life alone. Still she couldn't stop herself from asking. "Please, tell me your dream. Your whole dream."

He took a sip of coffee before beginning. "I was on your porch. You let me in." His eyes never left hers. "I kissed you, right there inside the door. I held you in my arms. I remember being able to feel you beneath your white cotton gown. You looked up at me with such..." He wanted to finish with the word *lust*. When he found there was no better word to describe the look in her eyes, he didn't go on right away.

"Such what?" she asked, trying to grasp at a memory she thought should be there. But she just couldn't find it. It was like trying to think of a certain word that is right on the tip of your tongue.

"Nothing," he said finally, with a slight shake of his head. His body was coming to life just thinking about it. "You made that comment about my making a trip to Port James. Then you told me my clothes were wet from the rain and that I should get out of them."

He paused and licked his lips. Kate nearly did the same, his words causing her mouth to turn dry. His words, combined with the sight of his tongue, reminded her of the dream. Just the thought of it filled her with a sudden flash of heat. She had to turn away from him for a moment for fear that he would be able to see it.

"You held my hand going up the stairs and helped me undress when we reached your bedroom. It's the big one at the end of the upstairs hall, isn't it?"

"Yes," Kate said curtly.

"I tore off two of the buttons on your gown trying to get it off. And when I finally did, I remember looking you up and down, thinking you were beautiful." He sounded a little embarrassed.

But Kate was paying little attention to his present emotions. She was too busy remembering. Her eyes narrowed with her increased concentration. "I remember that," she said slowly. "I remember you telling me that. And I said, 'No, I'm not.' And you said—"

"'Don't argue with me,'" he finished.

"You were wearing blue-and-white-striped boxer shorts," she added.

"I was yesterday," he said simply.

"What color are you wearing now?" Kate asked without thinking.

He stared at her in surprise. "I don't know," he replied, sounding rather exasperated. "What difference does it make?"

Kate set her cup on the table. She knew if she didn't, she'd soon spill it, her hands were shaking so much. She clenched her fists. "None." Her voice was tight.

Kate let it drop. "You carried me to the bed," she said, astonished. "No one has ever carried me to a bed before."

"Yes," he said softly, looking down into his cup of coffee as though it held the most interesting pictures. When his eyes shifted up again to meet hers, they were filled with brown, hazy smoke. "You're very sensitive near your hipbone," he pointed out.

The warmth of more blood rushed up her neck to her face. Her body responded as well with a tingling warmth in the pit of her stomach that swirled around and caused her nipples to grow taut, tightly pushing against the lacy roughness of her bra. Funny, that lace had never been uncomfortable until now.

"What do you think we should do?" she asked, trying to change the subject. She knew what she wanted to do. She knew what her body was crying out for her to do, and she ignored it. She clenched her fists again, tighter this time, to keep from reaching across the table to him. She intentionally avoided his eyes because she had the feeling that if she looked at him, he'd know it, too.

He shrugged. "I don't know." He absently rubbed the bridge of his nose as though he were very tired. "I should probably go back to Willows Point. I've got a lot of work to do there, but I just don't think I should get back behind the wheel without resting first."

"Willows Point?" The name sounded familiar to Kate, but she couldn't come up with a clear picture of it in her mind.

"It's about fifteen miles out of Bar Harbor," he explained.

Kate knew more of Bar Harbor. "You came all the way from Bar Harbor?" she asked. "That's a two-hour drive."

"Seven hours," he corrected, "if you don't know where you're going."

Kate's eyes widened. "Seven hours? You drove for seven hours?"

"I drove for four before I remembered Port James and headed in the right direction. I woke about seven-thirty, thinking of you, missing you. No matter how hard I tried, I couldn't go back to sleep," he explained. "My bed actually felt cold. Finally, I got up, threw on some clothes and went out to look for you."

"Seven-thirty," she muttered.

"That's when I woke."

"I woke up about that time, too, seven-thirty-four," she said slowly. "I was late. Either the alarm didn't go off, or I didn't hear it. And earlier this morning, at three minutes after five, I woke slightly. I felt you leave."

"That would give me a little more than two hours to drive home. Which is a little longer than it would take," he added. "But could I have done it in my sleep?"

Kate could only shrug. She was amazed they were discussing this all so calmly. She'd been known to talk about the weather with more emotion than this. She looked at Jake, studying him intently, trying to get past the handsome dark eyes and his rugged features, and see just how his brain worked, trying to picture him driving in his sleep to some little town fifteen miles out of Bar Harbor. No matter how hard she tried, she just couldn't see him doing it.

He stood up suddenly, as though something hot had touched him. Kate had the strange feeling he'd known she was trying to see him on the inside, and he didn't like it. "I'm going to go."

He ran his fingers through his hair, causing his waves to stand on end and reminding her of the way their lovemaking in her dream had done the same thing to her. He offered her a smile, the first one, and its brilliance caused her heart to skip a beat.

Kate forcefully swallowed down the lump in her throat it caused.

"I need to think without—" he stopped, but Kate knew what he nearly said. *Without Kate near him.* She understood the feeling, she, too, was finding it impossible to think coherently with him close to her.

"Me, too," she replied softly. The only problem was, she really didn't want to be left alone to think about anything. She had the feeling that the dream and knowing he shared it were going to fill most of her thoughts whether he were near or not. And she didn't want the fear that came along with those thoughts.

Kate got up and handed Jake his coat. His hand brushed against hers as he took it, and Kate pulled away quickly. But not quickly enough to stop the tingle that went up her arm. She saw him to the door. He paused, as if he wanted to say something. Kate had the oddest feeling that he was contemplating kissing her. She was wanting him to kiss her. She also found herself wishing he wouldn't leave. He seemed right, somehow, being in her house.

The next thing she knew, she was in his arms. The feeling was so familiar and so exciting at the same time. Everywhere his body touched hers, whether it was his naked hands or through his clothes, it left her feeling his heat. His lips came down on hers in a soft, gentle, caressing touch that caused her knees to almost give out beneath her. It brought back memories of their lovemaking dream with such a sudden intensity that Kate wanted to reach up to the buttons of his shirt. She couldn't even remember moving her arms, but she felt the soft cotton smoothness of his shirt beneath her palms. She had thought of touching him, and suddenly, she was. Her fingers were on his top button when she realized just what she was doing. With a soft moan, she tore herself away from him, out of his arms, away from his lips. Out from under the spell in which he'd held her.

With trembling fingers, Kate tentatively touched her own lips. With each breath, her fear of him grew. Had he hypnotized her? She couldn't remember having been so easily charmed before in her life. What would he have her doing next? Robbing banks? And she was trying hard to believe she'd actually experienced such a passionate kiss. Suddenly a scene flashed through her mind—it was the Fourth of July. But the fireworks had been in her mind . . . and throughout her body.

She held his gaze for a long time, and neither of them spoke. Only the sound of their breathing broke the silence. Kate wasn't sure, but she thought he looked just as surprised by the kiss as she felt.

Kate watched him turn suddenly and walk out the door without another word. Jake went down the steps, bowing his head against the rain. Even the way he walked was familiar to her. He climbed into his car, started it and turned on the wipers. Kate could see he was looking in her direction. She felt a sudden sense of loss that he was leaving and had to force herself away from the glass and return to her kitchen instead of running out on the porch to stop him. The desire to do just that was so strong, she even reached for the doorknob before turning away.

Her kitchen, the room where she always felt warm and at ease, suddenly felt cold and empty without him. A trace of Jake's musky, masculine scent lingered in the room. It was hauntingly familiar, and it made her miss him. She picked up his coffee cup and looked into it just as he had, as though she, too, were looking for answers there. She saw none, only the bit of cooling coffee he had left behind. She sighed deeply before taking the cup to the sink.

She needed to eat. She'd nearly developed an ulcer, thanks to the divorce, and she knew the importance of the right food at the right times. She just wished she didn't always have to force herself to eat. She wished she could enjoy food as she used to. But who wants to eat alone?

A bath was what she needed. A nice, hot bubble bath to warm away the rain and the cold, empty feeling she had. She would make herself a sandwich and eat in the tub. It was something she'd never done, but she now had the mad urge to do it.

Laughing out loud, Kate poured milk into a wineglass. So what if it wasn't champagne or something equally glamorous? She carried a tray to the upstairs bathroom and started water running in the tub.

She went into her room. Her bed was still unmade, her gown still lying on the floor. She picked it up absently, thinking she would put it on after her bath. She would start a fire in the fireplace and curl up on the sofa in front of the television. It all sounded like a perfect way to forget about the dream and to forget about Jake Casperson. She needed to forget them both. Thinking of either one reminded her of how lonely she felt most of the time. That was why she had chosen to teach in the first place. She'd needed to surround herself with a roomful of people, even if they were all only six years old.

She carried her gown to the bathroom and draped it over the back of the dressing chair. Looking down at it, she gasped.

The top two buttons were missing.

CHAPTER THREE

Jake drove to a bar and grill called Jerry's Place, located near the docks.

The rain continued steadily, and the smell of fish and salt hung heavily in the air as he made his way to the entrance.

The room he entered was smoke-filled and dark, smelling slightly of stale beer, perfume and several degrees of body odor all rolled into one.

It wasn't his kind of place, and Jake nearly walked out. He stopped himself. This was just the kind of place he needed. The kind of place where he could watch bets get placed on pool tables, listen to fish stories and forget. Forget about the woman he'd just left.

Leaving her had been hard in itself. Leaving her after that earth-moving kiss had been even harder. And not dragging her up the stairs to once again feel that patchwork quilt on her bed had been the hardest of all. He couldn't remember ever having wanted a woman more, ever having had even half the feelings for a woman that he did for Kate. He wanted her so bad, he ached. He actually ached. And no matter how hard he tried, he couldn't get her out of his mind. Everything he saw reminded him of something about her. His neck was a little stiff, and even that reminded him that he must have spent half the night with her, and half the day driving to reach her and then leave her.

He sat down at an empty table. A girl wearing tight jeans and an even tighter sweater came over. "Can I get you something, stranger?"

Jake looked up at her. Her body was young, she probably wasn't even thirty yet. She had long dark hair that was braided down her back. But her eyes were aged with lines and a certain look of experience.

"What's cooking tonight?" he asked.

"Shrimp and scallops, mostly. We usually have lobster, but the catch wasn't all that great today. We do have a good supply of cod, though." She smiled, showing a mouthful of crooked teeth.

Jake felt like something easy. "Get me whatever you've got that can be put into a sandwich," he said. "And a light beer."

"Do you want some fries with that?" She was writing on a small order pad.

"Sure, why not?"

He watched her walk off, maneuvering around the tables and customers. He found himself comparing her to Kate. Kate moved so much more fluidly, with the gracefulness of a ballet dancer, he thought. And he knew Kate's legs would look much more shapely in jeans than the waitress's did.

He leaned his elbows on the table and rested his head in his hands, letting out a sigh. Hell, what was happening to him? Had he really been with Kate, or had it all been a dream? If it had been a dream, it sure seemed pretty damned real to him. He knew more and remembered more than he had actually told her. He remembered the smell of her hair, so clean, and how soft it felt when he'd run his fingers through it. He remembered how he'd felt like laughing when he found that the soft curls between her legs were the same tawny color as the hair on top of her head.

He had to stop thinking about her. *He had to.* It only made him ache more.

The waitress set a tall mug of foamy beer in front of him and smiled before she moved off. He watched her only long enough this time to see one of the burly sailors at another table pat her backside as she walked by.

Jake took a big gulp of beer and wondered how many beers it would take to get him drunk enough to stop thinking about Kate. He realized he'd probably have to drink until he passed out. The beer was nearly gone by the time his sandwich arrived.

"Thanks," he muttered, looking down at the plate of breaded fish and fries. He suddenly had no desire to eat any of it.

"Another beer?" the waitress asked.

"Please."

He picked up a fry and stuffed it into his mouth. It tasted no better than sawdust. He wished he'd stayed at Kate's. The two of them could have shared the left-over tuna salad she had in her refrigerator.

He nearly choked on his fry. Where had that thought come from? He suddenly felt hot all over. He absently raked a hand through his hair. How the hell could he know she had tuna salad in her refrigerator? Yet, he did. He was certain of it.

He jumped up suddenly, nearly bumping into the waitress bringing his second mug of beer. Her sudden stop to avoid him caused the beer to slosh out over her hand and onto the floor.

"Hey!" she screeched.

He ignored her. "Have you got a phone?"

"Yeah, it's in the back." She pointed by holding her thumb in the direction of the area off to the side of the bar. "By the rest rooms."

"Is there a directory?"

"Yeah," she said again. "Hanging underneath."

He moved toward the phone.

"And don't be tearing out any of the pages, all right?" she nearly yelled after him.

He thought he heard her say something like "What a crazy..." but he ignored it. He reached the phone and grabbed the directory, opening it quickly to the *M*s.

Kate McCoy was the only McCoy. He read her number out loud, feeling as though it was now permanently embedded in his memory. He tossed a quarter into the phone and punched her number.

Her phone rang once.

Then a second time.

Then a third.

Why wasn't she answering? He knew she was there. He knew it, just as he knew there was tuna in her refrigerator. And he knew she wasn't asleep yet.

He closed his eyes, and he could see her. She was sitting in that living room with the violet wallpaper. She looked rosy and warm, and he nearly laughed when he saw she once again wore the white cotton gown with the two top buttons missing. He thought she had a fire burning in the fireplace.

She picked up the phone in the middle of the fourth ring. "Hello?" Her voice sounded relaxed and low, just as he remembered she'd spoken to him in the dream.

"Kate?"

She hesitated.

"Don't hang up," he said. He knew she wanted to. "Just tell—"

"Where are you?" she asked, interrupting him.

"Some bar and grill down near the docks," he replied absently.

"I'm not going to talk about the dream anymore," she said. "So don't ask me anything."

"Kate," he said. "I'm not going to ask you about the dream."

"Then what do you want?" she snapped.

He could see her standing in her kitchen, holding the phone to her ear. She was afraid. He could feel it. She was afraid of him, of what he was going to ask her. And she was afraid of herself. She was afraid of her thoughts and her feelings, and what she was thinking about Jake.

"Just tell me, do you have leftover tuna salad in your refrigerator, in a red plastic dish?"

She was quiet for several long seconds, and Jake had the feeling she didn't move, didn't even breathe.

"No," she replied finally, the one word coming out in a rush.

It was Jake's turn to be quiet. He knew she had tuna. He knew she was lying, and he knew she was doing it because she was afraid. He could see her standing there, rigid like a statue, biting her bottom lip. He wanted more than anything to calm her fear, to take her in his arms and tell her he was there for her. He could feel her needing him. He was needing her as well, maybe more.

"Don't call me anymore," she said suddenly. She was crying. Her voice shook.

"Kate—"

She hung up, and a dial tone touched his ear.

He muttered an oath and stared at the dead receiver in his hand. He shouldn't have called her. It had only frightened her more. He should have just gone back to her house and looked into her refrigerator himself. Then he would have been there to take her in his arms and help her deal with her fear. He was feeling the same fear. They could have dealt with it together. He hung up the phone.

Kate was still crying; he could hear her crying in his own mind. "I'm sorry, Kate," he mentally cried out to her, wondering if she could hear him like he could hear her. "I never wanted to hurt you."

Jake moved back to the table and his lonely-looking fried fish. He felt lost. He felt as though Kate and her house were home to him. As though Kate and everything she possessed had always been a part of him. Only now she didn't want him there, and he could no longer go to that home. But she did want him there, he thought. He knew she did. He could feel that, too. She was just afraid to want him there. He sat down and picked up his beer, looking at the foamy head for a moment. Seeing no answers there, he took a drink. Then he started to eat, not tasting a single bite.

Kate slammed down the phone and stared at it through tear-filled eyes. Why was he doing this to her? Just when she'd been able to get absorbed in a movie, he had to call and bring all her memories of him back to the surface of her mind where she didn't want them. Where she didn't need them.

She sniffed, bringing her crying under control, and shifted her gaze to the kitchen sink where she had placed the empty red container that had held her leftover tuna salad. She hadn't lied to him, not really. The tuna *had* been in there earlier, but she'd eaten it during her bath. So why did she feel that she'd lied to him? Why did she feel so guilty? And how could he possibly have known about it?

She reached into the cabinet for a mug. This time she was going to drink her milk warm. Perhaps it would help her sleep. She measured a mug of milk, poured it into a pan and placed it on her stove. She reached to turn on the flame beneath the pan and set the mug on the counter.

I'm sorry, Kate. I never wanted to hurt you.

The words popped into her mind with the suddenness of a lightning bolt.

Kate dropped the mug heavily on the counter. It was Jake's voice. He sounded so close, he could have been standing right behind her, whispering in her ear.

She was shaking. She felt as though she just might fall apart—again. "No!" she said out loud. She wouldn't let it happen again. She promised herself that she'd never, not ever, let another man hurt her. She'd never let another man make her feel that she was less than she was. Never. Never. Never!

She couldn't control this shaking. She thought her insides were trying to pull apart. She crossed her arms tightly, hoping it would help hold them together.

The milk started to boil, turning foamy and rising in the small pan. It reminded her of beer.

Why beer? She didn't even like beer.

She watched it continue to rise, and finally forced herself to turn off the stove just as the milk was about to boil over. What was happening to her? Was she losing her mind? Had she been losing it all these past months, and only now could see the actual signs of it happening? Was all of this just an overflow of emotions from the divorce? Dear God, she hoped not. The last thing she wanted to do was have to relive her nightmare of the divorce through some shrink.

She thought of every stress-handling maneuver she knew, and she used them all right now. Count to ten. Count to ten again, only take a deep breath between each number. She closed her eyes and put herself in a place where she felt relaxed. To Kate, it was a beach with her feet on the sand, the water rolling in and touching her toes.

She was not going to let this get to her, not as she had the divorce, not as she'd let the pain of her ex-husband's affair control her and nearly destroy her. She was stronger now. She was too strong to let this get to her. This was nothing more than a strange dream invading reality. By Monday, she'd be back to teaching, back to her normal life.

With a new wave of determination, she poured the milk into her mug and carried it back to the living room. She glued her eyes to the television and forced herself to concentrate on the movie she'd left, even though she could no longer even remember the plot.

She waited a few minutes for her milk to cool before she took a sip. Again, the bubbly top reminded her of beer.

She watched the television, trying to ignore the way the man on the screen reminded her of Jake. She didn't want to think of him at all. She never wanted to see Jake Casperson again. He was too good-looking, with his hair reminding her of dark honey. Kate closed her eyes, but she still saw Jake. He seemed dangerous, the type of man who always had women tripping over themselves to be near him. Younger women. Kate didn't want to deal with that. She'd had that before, and she never wanted it again.

She quickly opened her eyes, trying to watch the movie. To her amazement, it was over. She had been so preoccupied, she hadn't even realized the movie had ended, the plot complete.

The local news came on, and it was just what Kate needed to put her to sleep. She stayed awake only long enough to finish her milk.

She didn't even realize she was falling asleep. She merely crossed over to the other side of consciousness where dreams took over.

Two miles away, Jake Casperson checked into a motel, wanting only to take a shower and fall into bed. He felt as if he'd been up for days, instead of hours. After a good night's sleep and a big breakfast, he planned to get back to Willows Point—where his work could fill his mind and he could forget about Kate McCoy.

CHAPTER FOUR

"Kaitlan."

She woke at the sound of her name and smiled up at him. She felt the soft caress of his fingers against her cheek.

"You left your front door open," he said. He leaned over her and gently placed his warm lips on hers. "That could be dangerous. You wouldn't want a stranger coming in."

"I knew you'd be coming," she said softly. "And you're the strangest man I know." She laughed softly at her own joke. He smiled down at her.

The lights were off. The television was off. The only light came from the burning embers of the fire in the fireplace, and still, she could see him clearly. Even more clearly than the previous night.

His lips returned to hers just as his arms moved to scoop her up against his chest. She could feel his heart beating. "Where are we going?" she asked, pulling away.

"Right down here in front of the fire."

He set her down gently, and Kaitlan recognized the feel of the patchwork quilt off her bed.

He reached for the hem of her gown and pushed it up her legs, enabling his hands to caress her skin in the process. He left an instant trail of fire where he touched her. "I'm tired of having to remove this in order to see you," he said, his voice deep and husky. "And touch you. I think I'll toss it into the fire right now and be rid of it."

She chuckled again at his words just as his fingers lightly crossed over her hipbone. And her chuckle turned instantly into a full-fledged squealed giggle.

He chuckled, as well, at her response. "You're very sensitive tonight, aren't you?"

She didn't have to admit it, he already knew.

He slid out of his shirt, never taking his eyes from her. Kaitlan reached up and pulled the snap of his jeans free, unzipping them before she eased them down. Seductively, she laughed. "Red, I should have guessed."

"Red, like a hot fire," he whispered, slipping off his shorts. There was fire in his eyes as well. His hands moved to her then. "Now, let's find out where else you're sensitive." He began his search for sensitive spots with his fingers and his lips. His touch set a fire inside her, burning hotter than the flames in the fireplace. And that fire soon threatened to consume her.

"I love you, Kaitlan," he whispered into her ear.

"Show me how much, Jacob."

He slipped into her warmth, making himself a part of her. "Your wish is my command, sweet thing."

Jake woke to the pounding.

Someone was pounding on the door to his motel room. Why the hell did it sound like the door was right next to his head? He closed his eyes tighter against the noise. The last thing he wanted to do was wake up. Even half awake, half asleep, he recognized the feeling of exhaustion, and he knew that one night's sleep obviously wasn't enough. His head hurt, and his neck felt stiff. He couldn't understand why. He'd only drunk three beers last night, knowing that no amount of alcohol was going to make him stop wanting Kate McCoy.

The pounding continued. His head didn't need it.

"Leave me alone!" he called out. He surely didn't need his own yelling, either. It caused his head to throb. He attempted to roll over and draw the pillow over his head as a barrier against the noise. Until he realized there was no pillow. That realization brought him more to the side of wakefulness. It also brought about the realization that he wasn't in a bed. And he wasn't in the motel room where he'd gone to sleep.

He was in a car. His car. And the pounding was being done by someone's fist on the window right next to him. He opened his eyes wide and tried to focus. It was a man in a blue uniform beating on his window.

A policeman.

Jake uttered an oath and reached to roll down the window. The air that came in through that small opening was cold and damp, but there was no actual rain. The light of morning seemed unusually bright despite the lack of sun, and it hurt his eyes. If he hadn't known better, he'd have thought someone had just stuck an ice pick through one of his eyes and pierced his brain for all the pain he was feeling.

"Step out of the car, please," the officer said firmly.

Jake hesitated only a moment while trying to get his bearings. Damn, he wasn't even sure where he was. But that changed immediately as he climbed out and looked around.

He was parked in front of Kate's house.

Kate was standing on her porch, wearing a coat over her white nightgown. She had on red fuzzy slippers, and her eyes were wide with fear. Her face was pale.

And still, he thought she was beautiful. She held her arms crossed over herself as though she might be freezing to death. Her eyes were glued to him.

"Do you have some identification?" The policeman drew his attention away from Kate.

"Y-yes," he stammered, reaching for his wallet. He pulled out his driver's license.

The policeman took it and studied it. "Would you mind telling me why you're parked in front of Ms. McCoy's house, sleeping in your car?"

"We, ah..." He didn't quite know how to go on. He looked back at Kate. Her hair was all tousled. Their night together—or was it just another dream—flashed through his mind in a wave that nearly knocked him off his feet. "We had a misunderstanding, officer," he said, forcing his voice to stay even. "I left, and I came back to apologize. I guess I was afraid to approach her just yet and I fell asleep. I've been doing a lot of driving lately, and I think it caught up with me."

"She said she didn't know you," the policeman said.

Jake glanced at the man. The name tag below his badge read Hewer.

"Well, Officer Hewer," he said, "she does know me. Tell him you know me, Kate," he yelled up to her.

Kate colored visibly, a lovely shade of pink rose from her neck to her face. Her rich, full mouth turned down slightly. Even from this distance, her lips looked swollen from his kisses. Damn, if he didn't have the urge to kiss her again.

"You obviously know her first name," said Hewer.

"I know her intimately," Jake replied loud enough for Kate to hear. "And we had a misunderstanding, that's all."

"A misunderstanding?" asked Hewer. He looked back at Kate, having to turn slightly to do so.

"Yes," Jake replied easily. "And I think she called you because she was angry at me, that's all."

"Well..." Hewer looked slightly embarrassed. "I hope you folks will be able to work it out." He obviously assumed it was nothing more than a lovers' spat.

"We'll do our best." Jake offered Hewer his best I'm-a-real-nice-guy smile. "I'm just sorry your time was wasted."

"She's a nice lady," said Hewer. "My sister's little girl is in her class."

"Yes," replied Jake, "she is a nice lady." He said it a little louder than normal, too, glancing at Kate. She was glaring at him. Jake also emphasized the word *nice,* giving it a little more meaning than the policeman had.

"Well, listen," said Office Hewer. "I'm sorry about this. She didn't tell me you two knew each other."

"It's all right, I understand," Jake said, his voice smooth. He was holding his smile so tight, his face was beginning to hurt as much as the rest of his head.

Hewer turned back toward his car. It was enough to bring Kate down the steps of the porch. "You're leaving?" she questioned. "Aren't you going to arrest him?"

He turned to her. "On what charge, Ms. McCoy?"

"I don't know," she snapped back. "Isn't it illegal to sleep in front of someone else's house?"

Officer Hewer shrugged. "No, I don't believe so. Now, had he been in your drive, I suppose that would be trespassing. But he's on the side of the street, and that's public property," he explained.

"Harassment, then," Kate put in.

This time Hewer sighed loudly. "And just what has he done to harass you?"

"He—" she started. There was nothing else she could say. If she told Hewer Jake invaded her dreams at night and made passionate love to her until she screamed, he'd probably send out the men in white coats who carried straitjackets. She could definitely forget about her job then.

"I offer her a greater challenge than she's had in a long time," finished Jake. His lips shifted into a half grin, and if looks could really kill, Kate would have had him dead by now. Her eyes were shooting daggers at him. He noticed something else, looking into them. They were red and puffy, as though she'd had a lot to drink the night before or she didn't get much sleep, either. Jake had the feeling his eyes didn't look much better.

"Why don't you just leave, Jake?"

He smiled that nice-guy smile again, this time at Kate. "I don't want to, Kate. We need to work things out."

She opened her mouth to speak, but Officer Hewer stopped her. "I think I'll leave this to you two," he said. This time he was able to make it to his car and open the door before Kate stopped him.

"He's a dangerous man, officer."

Hewer's gaze met hers evenly. "How so, Ms. McCoy?"

"I have reason to believe he broke into my house last night while I was asleep."

Hewer's brows rose on that one. "He did?"

"I did not," said Jake hotly. With his growing anger, it was taking everything he had to keep his voice under control. Damn! None of this was his fault. Why was she doing this to him? The answer came to him just as quickly as the question. *Because she's afraid.*

Officer Hewer looked up toward Kate's house. "What makes you think he broke in? Is there a lock or a window broken?"

"No, I—" she started again and stopped.

Jake knew exactly what she'd started to say. "Tell him, Kate," Jake said.

She colored again. Her obvious embarrassment cooled his anger in an instant.

"Tell me what?" Hewer was serious.

She looked from one man to the other, her color increasing. "I knew he'd be back. I left the door open." With that, she turned and headed back up the steps of her front porch. The white ruffle of her gown rose slightly with her movement, revealing her calf above her red fuzzy slippers. She went into the house and slammed the front door.

Hewer looked back at Jake. "Looks like you certainly have your work cut out for you. I don't envy you."

"Thanks a lot," muttered Jake, his eyes still on the front door. Officer Hewer didn't know the half of it. He was thinking it was a simple little quarrel. Jake wondered what Hewer would think if he told him everything.

"Can I give you some advice?"

Jake looked at Hewer. The man was tall, with massive shoulders that looked as if he worked out and took a few steroids every now and then. Jake had to look up slightly to meet his eyes. "What?"

"Send her some flowers. It always softens them enough so you can talk to them. I've had to do it a few times with my wife."

Jake thought of the rose he'd brought yesterday. It came to him what Kate had done with it after he left. It was in a vase on her kitchen table. "Thanks." He gave Hewer one more smile and moved away, heading toward the house. He knew Kate was waiting for him. At the front door, he turned and waved to Hewer. Then he went inside.

Kate was waiting for him, just as he thought, at the kitchen table. She was leaning her head on the palm of one hand. She looked lost. She'd hung her coat on a peg near the back door. Jake took off his own and hung it beside hers.

"Kate," he said gently, sitting down across from her in the same chair he had been in the previous night, that single pink rose between them.

"My living room is a wreck," she said softly, without looking at him.

"I know. We, ah, got a little wild, didn't we?" His mouth was dry. He licked his lips.

"Did we?" she asked, her voice hardly more than a whisper. "Did we really? Or was it just another dream?"

"I think I was here." He never took his eyes from her. He felt her fear so strong, he hurt with it. "I'm almost sure I was here."

"How?"

"I don't know," he answered honestly. "I only know that with each passing minute, I know more about you than I did the minute before."

Kate said nothing. She didn't even look at him.

Jake went on. "I know your favorite color is peach. I know about your divorce."

Her eyes met his at that.

"I know that when you were packing to come here, you found your wedding album. You sat for a long time looking at it. Then you slowly tore up every picture in it."

"Is this some sort of government experiment?" she asked, straightening for the first time.

"I wish I knew. I feel like I know everything else."

"I know," she said slowly. "I feel the same way. It's like I know everything about you, but I'd never seen you before yesterday." She got up.

"What are you going to do?" he asked, watching her closely.

"Fix breakfast." She moved to the refrigerator, her movements slow and automatic. "Your favorite. Ham and scrambled eggs." She pulled out two eggs and moved to the counter near the stove, where she promptly dropped them both. They broke on the tile floor, each with a splat, the yolks an immediate mess.

"Kate?" He rose quickly and moved to her.

The blank look on her face frightened him. She stood staring down at the broken eggs. When she didn't answer, he took her arm and shook her slightly, until she looked up at him. "Kate."

"It started before yesterday," she said slowly. "It started before that first dream."

"Are you sure?" He felt her fear. His own was rippling through him as well.

She nodded. "I bought the ham at the grocery store Wednesday night. I don't eat much ham. I seldom buy it."

"It's too salty," he said knowingly.

She nodded again.

"What did you think when you bought it?" he asked, his fear growing.

"I don't remember thinking anything." She looked as if she might cry, and she took a few deep breaths. "I walked past the meat cooler, picking up the things I normally buy. And I saw this small ham. I remember thinking that it was just the right size. I picked it up and I put it in the cart. I paid for it, and that's all."

"Just the right size?" Jake let go of her, walked to the refrigerator and opened it. He pulled out the small ham and looked at it. "Just the right size for what?" he asked, looking down at it. It was nothing more than a plain, ordinary, little chunk of ham.

"Just the right size for two people," she replied.

CHAPTER FIVE

"What were *you* doing?" Kate asked.

"What?" Jake looked up at her, as though the sound of her voice surprised him. He was still holding the chunk of ham, looking down at it as if it were going to do tricks in his hand or something.

"Wednesday night, when I was picking out a ham that was just right. What were you doing?"

She was looking at him, feeling rather calm. She felt his fear as well as her own, and for some reason the two of them being together in their fear was somewhat comforting.

"Rearranging the furniture in my boat."

"A houseboat," she said. It wasn't a question. She already knew it was true.

"Yes." He finally set the ham on the counter, coming closer to her. Their eyes met. He reached out and grasped her hand in an unexpected gesture that caused her pulse to quicken.

"Why?" she asked. "Why were you rearranging the furniture?"

"It just seemed too crowded. There wasn't enough room." His eyes looked like dark fire.

Kate knew that, too. "Not enough room for two people," she said. It was another statement, not a question.

He looked down at her. She was wearing only her white nightgown, which was still missing the top two buttons. Kate closed her eyes for several seconds. "So were you here or weren't you?"

Jake sighed loudly, finally releasing her hand. He grabbed a paper towel and bent to wipe up the mess of broken eggs near her feet, feet still wrapped in fuzzy red slippers. "I think the first night was a dream. I don't know. It's hard for me to believe I drove two hundred miles in my sleep. But last night I think I was really here. Oh, I don't know."

Kate laughed sarcastically. "How are we supposed to practice safe sex when we're not sure if it's real or not?"

He paused in his mission of cleaning to look up at her. Seeing her grin, he matched it. "Hell if I know," he muttered.

She knelt beside him, their faces close. She could feel his breath, smell the masculine scent that she now recognized as his own. Her face grew serious, her eyes pleading. "What do you suppose is happening to us, really?"

Jake wanted to kiss her and tell her everything was going to be all right. Damn, forget about reassuring her. He simply wanted to kiss her. But he knew she was still afraid of so many things. Jake was afraid, too, and he felt her fear nearly as much as he felt his own. He didn't have the vaguest idea as to how to start explaining any of this. Not to her. Not to himself.

He shrugged. "I wish I knew. I feel like something has linked me to you. Something that was strong enough to draw me in your direction and lead me here." He scratched his head absently. "I don't know what the hell it was. I only know it's strong enough to give me feelings for you that I've never shared with any other woman.'' It sounded like the biggest pickup line he'd ever heard, even to his own ears. But it didn't seem to faze Kate. Her determined expression never changed.

''Do you think it could be some sort of government experiment, like you read about in science fiction books?'' Kate asked.

''Have you noticed anybody watching you?'' he asked, avoiding a direct answer. He stood for a moment to get more towels. Then he knelt again where the soft woman scent of her touched him. He closed his eyes briefly, hoping that not seeing her could convince him that she wasn't nearly as close to him as he knew she was. It didn't work. Damn, he wanted her. He couldn't even believe how much.

''No, why?'' She was looking right at him, only inches away. And she couldn't seem to see the agony he was experiencing.

''Don't you think if it was something run by the government they would be keeping tabs on us, watching our every move?'' His voice was tight, his throat dry.

Kate paused. Had she finally noticed how much he wanted her? he wondered. Her reply told him she obviously hadn't.

''I suppose so. I never thought about it before.''

Jake finished wiping up the eggs with a final, frustrated swipe. And both of them stood up, nearly bumping heads they moved so close.

''Why do you call me Kaitlan?'' she asked.

She still hadn't noticed the way his body was calling out for her, or she was ignoring it if she had. He supposed he should feel grateful, but he wasn't.

"Probably the same reason you call me Jacob," he replied, throwing the messy paper towels into the trash under her sink. He didn't have to ask where the trash was, he already knew. And moving away from her brought him some relief, although not much.

"Isn't that your full name?" She watched him another moment before unwrapping the chunk of ham.

"Yes, but I think the last time I heard it was when I was twelve and my mother caught me sneaking a cigarette. What about you—is Kaitlan your name?" he asked, thinking that it had to be. He was still standing close to her. He stayed for another moment before moving to the refrigerator to get new eggs. Kate went about slicing the ham into thick pieces.

"Yes, but even my mother doesn't call me that. Only Mr. Taylor, who lives down the street, calls me Kaitlan," she replied, without looking up from her slicing.

"Mr. Taylor?"

"He's an old man who lives at the end of the block. He's supposed to be a hundred years old this year." It was nice to talk about something else for the moment.

"And he lives alone?" Jake asked.

"Yes," she replied. "He used to be a sailor years ago. Now he just stays there, and we, all of his neighbors, sort of take care of him. We bring him meals, check up on him, things like that."

Jake was watching her closely. He thoroughly enjoyed watching her, and he felt he would probably never grow tired of doing it. "Why isn't he in a home?"

Kate smiled. "He refuses to leave. He says this is his home. And it's where his garden is. The man lives for his garden. You should see the roses he grows. He wins awards every year, and there's even been a few magazine articles about his roses. He also says that being there keeps him close to his one true love, but he's never told any of us just who his one true love is. The only way he's leaving it is when he's carted off to the cemetery."

Jake laughed. "Sounds like my kind of man. And he calls you Kaitlan?"

"Yes." She paused in her slicing. "Do you suppose it could be something unnatural?" she asked, jumping back to the subject of their dreams. She was surprised at how calm they both were about this.

"Unnatural?"

He said the word as though he'd never heard it before and didn't know its true meaning. "The *attraction* feels natural," he admitted, going on. "Like it's something we're supposed to do. But the fact that it's happening at all seems pretty unnatural to me."

"I meant like ghosts or spirits or things not of this world," she said, reaching into the cabinet for a skillet.

"Are there sexual spirits?" he asked, setting three eggs on the counter near her. He was close again. He didn't move away. He simply leaned against the counter there, watching her heat the ham.

"I've heard of something called an incubus. It's sexual, and it comes upon people in their sleep."

"Maybe that's what we've got," he said.

It was Kate's turn to shrug. "I don't know. I heard about it on the radio around Halloween. You know. When they put on all the scary stuff they can find. Anyway—" she paused to flip the ham "—they had on the radio some ghost hunter or someone, who was talking about this girl who conjured up a spirit with some kid's game. But it was aggressive. Every time she went to sleep, it came to her and hurt her. In physical ways."

"What we have sure isn't by any means aggressive." He looked right at her. "I haven't hurt you, have I?" He could bet his bottom dollar he hadn't, but he still had to ask.

It was a full minute before she answered, and she felt her body grow hot just thinking about it. "No," she replied, without looking at him.

He drove her to the ends of the sane world as she knew it. He made her beg and cry and feel she was quivering with need and breaking into thousands of pieces inside. But he never hurt her. She blushed just thinking about it, and she kept her face turned toward the stove to keep him from seeing it. Even though she had the feeling, he didn't have to look at her to see it.

"Jake?" she asked softly.

"Yes?"

She could feel his eyes on her. "Did you really put me on the coffee table last night?"

He didn't answer her right away. In fact, he never actually answered her question. "You're going to burn it," he said, talking about the ham.

Kate turned the ham with a fork and lowered the heat, wishing she could lower her own heat and forget about the previous night the same way. He was making her feel like some teenager going through puberty whose hormones were beyond control. And she didn't like the feeling. Since the divorce, she'd meant to remain in full control of everything regarding her own life. Keeping that control in this instance wasn't possible.

Jake got a bowl and another fork. He knew exactly where she kept things. He broke the eggs into the bowl and whipped them without speaking.

"What do you think we should do?" Kate asked before grabbing a plate for the ham.

He added milk to the eggs and a few drops of vanilla. Just the way Kate liked them. "I don't know what we *should* do, I only know what I want to do," he replied, looking up at her.

Kate looked at him. He wanted to kiss her again. She knew that, she could see that. Even though she felt as if he was talking about something else. "Which is what?" She forced herself to ask, her mouth suddenly dry. It was impossible for her to look away from him.

"Take you back to Willows Point with me," he said simply. His eyes were still telling her he wanted to kiss her.

Kate stepped away from the stove without his asking her so he could pour the eggs into the skillet.

"I have work there," he went on, his concentration now on cooking the eggs. But was his voice lower, huskier?

"And I have work here," she put in.

"But I think it's a good idea for us to stay together as much as we can," he said, still looking away from her.

"Why?" Kate started fixing coffee without asking if he wanted any. She felt the same way, though. She just didn't want to admit it to herself.

"I don't know. I just do. Unless," he paused, "you don't want to come with me." He still wasn't looking at her.

Kate both wanted to go with him, and didn't want to go with him, if that was possible. "But my job," she said again. It was the only excuse she had.

She felt she should be with him. It felt right to be with him. She felt that he was a very important part of her life and that she knew him almost better than she knew herself.

At the same time, she didn't want to get close to him. The divorce had burned her terribly, and she kept telling herself the last thing she wanted was another man who might hurt her.

"I can promise you I won't hurt you," he said, reading her mind.

It didn't even bother her that he'd known what she was thinking. Nor did it surprise her. At that point in time, Kate thought if aliens came down in a red spaceship with blinking lights and landed in her backyard, she still wouldn't have been surprised. "How can you promise that?"

He turned and met her gaze, holding her eyes. Green met brown with a combination of strength and fire, as though their souls were meeting and locking together in a single look.

"I just can," he replied.

Kate chuckled bitterly. "You can? You make this all sound so simple. Like some knight in shining armor on a white stallion riding in to take me away. And what happens when a cute, younger woman comes along and you start to have these wild dreams with her?" she snapped.

"That won't happen."

Her chuckle turned into a full laugh. "It won't?" Her eyes never left his. "I've seen it happen. I've felt it happen. There isn't any way you can assure me that someday you wouldn't come home from a hard day's work and say, 'Honey, I've been having an affair and I've fallen in love with her.'" That was almost exactly what David had told her. "Or better yet, you could say that you've been having these really wild dreams with some pretty little blonde and you want to go see if you can find where she lives because you don't know if the dreams are real or not."

"That won't happen," he said again, forcefully this time.

"How do you know?" She was nearly screaming at him.

He didn't answer her question. "Tell me, Kate," he said, "why did you marry him in the first place?"

His question startled her. "What?"

"And don't tell me it was because you loved him. You probably did. You'd known him all your life, you'd grown up with him. He was dependable, he was familiar. He was a very good friend of your family. Isn't that right?"

Kate stood unable to move, hardly able to breathe. Everything he said was true. "How do you know all that?" The question was no more than a whisper.

"The same way I know everything else. And that isn't all, is it? You were hurt when he cheated on you, weren't you?"

"Yes," she whispered, still unable to tear her gaze from his.

"But it wasn't because you loved him, was it?"

This time Kate didn't answer.

"It was because you felt betrayed."

She still said nothing.

"And during the divorce, you weren't hurting because of any great love for him. You were hurting because he had someone and he was leaving you alone. You were hurting because you felt like you'd failed." He took a step closer. "But it wasn't really because you loved him."

"Shut up!" she yelled in his face.

She turned her back on him, breaking the hold he'd had on her with his gaze. Tears came to her eyes. And she refused, absolutely refused to let them fall. She'd die before she cried over David or the divorce again. She had made that promise to herself months ago. Still, everything Jake said was true. She'd never felt so invaded in her life. She took a deep breath, then another, then another and another. It was the only thing she knew to do to keep from falling apart.

She felt his hands on her shoulders. "Tell me something else, Kate." His breath was near her ear.

She was suddenly leaning back on him, feeling his entire body pressing against her, feeling his strength. It reminded her of the way he held her after making love with her, whether it was a dream or not. It felt so good to be held, to not have to fight alone.

"Did he ever make you feel the way you feel with me when we make love?"

His words were quiet, warm against her ear. His whole body was warm against her. "Did he ever make you scream or cry or beg?" he asked. "Did you two ever destroy your living room like we did?"

Kate sniffed, her need to cry disappearing with his touch, with the way he was holding her. She'd never felt so safe, so secure in her life. At the same time, his being there, so close, was sending her emotions into a tug-of-war. She found it impossible to lie to him. "No," she replied so softly, he could hardly hear her.

Yet he didn't need to hear her. He already knew the answer. "And even though you grew up with him, do you think you knew as much about him as you know about me? Do you think you were as linked to him as you feel linked to me?"

"No," she whispered again.

"Then how can you think things would be the same with me? You'd be lying to me and to yourself if you thought they would be."

"I know," she said in a small voice. "I know." She closed her eyes, wanting only to feel him against her, wanting to feel his sureness, the certainty of him. His arms came around her, holding her in something like a bear hug with his arms pressed against her breasts.

"Will you come with me?" he asked softly after a moment.

She wondered again if he was hypnotizing her. "You make it sound so easy," she said slowly. "As if it means nothing to simply pack a few things and go with you wherever you want to take me. You could be a serial killer planning to slash my throat for all I know." She turned and looked at him.

He was so close, and he offered her a small grin. "You of all people know I'm not."

"So what about my life? I have a job teaching small children in this town. And I promised Mr. Taylor that I'd be by this morning to check on him. And I'm supposed to go shopping with my friend Maddie this morning." Teaching, her few friends, Mr. Taylor, antique hunting had all been aspects of her life for the past year. So why did they suddenly sound so empty when they'd held her together for the past year?

"I know," was all Jake would reply.

There was a long silence between them. Kate didn't know what else to say to convince him how important these things were to her. Looking into his eyes just then, she didn't feel too convinced herself.

"I'll bring you back tomorrow afternoon. Is that soon enough?" Jake asked finally. His voice was low and husky again. It entered her ear with a tingle that moved through her body.

He made it sound so nice. The room was silent for a moment. "I think our eggs are burning," she said then, unable to give him a definite answer just yet.

He let her go and turned to the stove. "They're not too bad." He turned it off and spooned the eggs onto plates with the ham. Kate poured their coffee. They sat down at the table opposite each other.

They ate in nearly total silence. It was while they drank their second cups of coffee that the conversation started up again.

"So if I do go with you, how would we go about finding out what's going on?" Kate asked.

"I wish I knew." Jake's eyes met hers evenly. "I just think we should stay together as much as possible. I know more about you as time goes on, and I think you know about me, too. Maybe after enough time, we'll know why and what and how. Not to mention, I don't like the idea of doing any more driving in my sleep."

"We'll actually be spending the night together tonight if I go with you. I mean, it's a night that we're certain of." Kate's words were slow. The thought of spending the night with him frightened her nearly as much as the dreams. For the first time, she wasn't sure what Jake must be thinking. Did he think that she was easy because of the dreams or whatever they were? Did he think he could take her back to his boat and two of them could destroy his living quarters as they had her living room?

He knew what she was thinking. He knew her fears. He reached across the table and took her hand. "Kate, we'll take this slow. We'll take each day—and night—as it comes, and we'll deal with what happens as it happens. I'm not going to push you into something you're not ready for."

Kate could see he meant it, every word. "I don't know why I believe you, but I do. Especially after all those... things you got me to do with you last night." No matter how hard she tried, she couldn't keep their time together out of her mind. She took a final long sip of her coffee to hide the blush she felt rise to her cheeks, then set down the cup. "The houseboat you live on is big, isn't it?" she asked, trying to change the subject.

"Yes."

She'd thought as much. It was as if that thought were a memory from long ago, yet it wasn't quite clear.

"I'll go with you."

She heard his sigh.

"On two conditions," she continued. "That if I want to come home at any time, for any reason, you'll bring me back."

Jake's gaze held hers from across the table. "And the second?"

She noticed right away that he didn't readily agree to the first one. "That you have me back by seven tomorrow evening."

At that one, he nodded. "All right."

"I'll be back in a few minutes. I need to get dressed and pack." She got up.

"Take your time," he muttered, his back to her. "I'll have another cup of coffee."

"You could go with me to see Mr. Taylor," she suggested. "If you'd like," she added hesitantly. For some reason, seeing Mr. Taylor seemed like an oddly intimate thing to share with Jake. It reminded her a little of taking her date home to meet her parents.

"I'd like that," he replied softly.

At the doorway she stopped and watched him refill his cup. "Maybe it's aliens from outer space," she suggested, going back again to the subject of the dreams. It seemed that no matter how often or far they strayed from that subject, it was impossible to actually avoid it. Kate thought it was probably because the fear never seemed to leave.

Jake choked at her words and spit his coffee. Kate seemed barely to notice his action, even with all the coughing he did. "Aliens?" he questioned when he was finally able to speak clearly.

"Why not?" she asked. "It's as good an explanation as any of the others."

Jake watched her for a long moment. There was something so innocently beautiful about her expression, he didn't quite know what else to do but look at her. "I guess. Maybe you're right," he said finally, even though he didn't believe a word of it.

She smiled at him softly, and it was nearly enough to cause him to cross the room and feel that sweet mouth against his own. She turned away then, and it took every ounce of his willpower not to stop her.

Kate went upstairs, deliberately ignoring her living room as she walked past the doorway. In her room, she ignored the unmade bed as well, and the fact that the quilt her mother made, which had never been out of this room since she'd brought it in, was not there. She grabbed a large tote bag and threw in some toiletries, jeans, two heavy sweaters and underclothes. She changed into a third large sweater and another pair of jeans, a pair of heavy socks and her sneakers.

She turned around and gasped to find Jake standing in the doorway, her quilt folded in his arms. How long had he been standing there? She hadn't even heard him come up.

"I put the cushions back on the sofa and moved the coffee table back," he said. "I hope you don't mind."

"N-no. Thanks," she stammered. She really was grateful. It saved her from having to go in and do it. She took the quilt from him, her hands shaking. She set it on the bed, feeling his eyes watching her every move. For a moment, Kate wondered about her decision to go with him. But she said nothing. She was no longer thinking right or wrong. She knew only that she wanted to be with Jake for some unknown reason. And that realization hit her with enough impact to nearly knock the breath out of her.

Jake, too, said nothing. He merely picked up her bag and followed her out to his car, where he put her bag into the back seat.

They walked hand in hand down the block to another large Victorian house. Kate knocked, then entered through the front door. "Mr. Taylor?" she called out. "It's me, Kate."

Jake followed her past the stairs into the living room. The television was showing men's downhill skiing on some sports program.

Jake stopped just inside the living room door, feeling somewhat out of place. He could see the top of Mr.

Taylor's head as he sat in a large recliner. The back of the recliner faced Jake.

"Is that you, Kaitlan dear?" came the old man's scratchy voice.

"Yes." She moved around the recliner where he could see her, and she knelt beside the arm of the chair.

Jake saw the head of thinning silver hair turn to face her. A hand with clawlike fingers patted Kate's hand.

"Did you have any breakfast?" Kate asked.

"I fixed myself some toast," the old man replied. "Even spread the butter and jelly on myself."

Kate smiled up at him. "That's great. Mrs. Blume next door said she was going to fix a big pot of stew and bring you some today. Do you remember?"

"Of course I remember," he snapped. "My body may be worn out, but my brain works just like it did when I was young."

Kate smiled patiently. And Jake smiled at her kindness.

"I know, you're right," she said to Mr. Taylor. "I'm going out of town for the weekend. Is there anything I can get you before I go."

"No, no." The hand with the clawlike fingers waved her away. "I'm fine. I'll just sit here and watch television." He paused. "But where's your manners, dear Kaitlan? You've brought someone with you, and you never introduced us."

Kate stood up. "I'm sorry." At her motion, Jake came farther into the room where Mr. Taylor could see him.

"Mr. Jonathan Taylor, this is my friend—"

"I know who you are," Mr. Taylor snapped, interrupting with such hostility that all Kate could do was stare at him. It was obvious he thought Jake was someone else from his past.

"You do?" Jake was just as surprised as Kate. "Well, Kate's told me about you, too, and may I say I'm honored to meet—"

"No, you may not say anything. Now take yourself the hell out of my house and stay out!"

Kate didn't know what to do. Her eyes shifted from one man to the other in confusion.

"I'll wait outside," Jake said finally, much to Kate's relief.

Kate followed him within minutes. "I don't understand why he did that," she said. "He obviously thought you were someone else, but I don't have the vaguest idea who. And he wouldn't tell me."

"Has he ever done that with anyone else?" Jake asked. They walked back toward Kate's house, to his car.

She took his hand without thinking. "Yes, he thinks Mrs. Blume's daughter is someone named Lilia, but her name is really Joan."

Jake chuckled. "Well, then we'll just forget it and pass it off as the ramblings of an old man. Besides, we have other things to think about. Are you ready?" he said as he opened his car door.

"I guess." Kate climbed in, wondering if she was ready. Ready to face whatever might be ahead for the two of them.

CHAPTER SIX

Jake's houseboat was large, docked in the harbor among several others.

Kate admired it in awe. "It's really big," she said, more to herself than to him.

Jake climbed aboard via the gangplank, then turned back to her. "It didn't seem so Wednesday night." He held out his hand to her.

Kate smiled up at him a moment before placing her hand into the warmth of his. He didn't let go of her even after she was aboard, and his hand felt too warm, too strong for Kate to pull away. The boat gently rocked in the waves, giving a lulling effect that Kate liked. Jake led her through a glass door into the living room. One entire wall was glass—all windows, giving a spectacular view of the other boats and the ocean. It was like looking at a life-size postcard.

"It's beautiful," Kate whispered. She was vaguely aware that Jake was still holding her hand.

"It's one reason why I bought it. I used to rent a place right in the center of Willows Point, and I couldn't stand it. It was a little hole-in-the-wall apartment, and it seemed like all the windows looked out on the bricks of the buildings around it. I'd come down here as much as I could just to see the ocean, to get rid of the closed-in feeling the apartment gave me. Then I saw this for sale." Jake was speaking without looking at her. He was looking, as she was, out the windows at the water. "I think I signed the papers for it that same day."

There was a moment of comfortable silence. Jake was still holding her hand, and Kate felt closer to him at that moment than she had ever felt to another human being. Holding his hand, looking at the eternity of the ocean, she felt like he'd just shared a very intimate secret with her. She slowly turned to look at him, only to find him gazing at her. Her heart did a sudden somersault. She would never have believed that such tenderness, such feeling, such an acute sense of caring could be communicated in a man's eyes, in his expression. She didn't understand the why of it or the how, but she did understand what Jake had meant when he'd said he felt linked to her.

Kate didn't remember either of them moving, yet suddenly they were standing close, facing each other. He leaned toward her, his lips touching hers softly. The impact, however, was far from soft. The touch started an instant fire within her, a fire that threatened to consume her within seconds. Her whole being responded to him in that same moment. She pressed herself against him, and he welcomed her response by wrapping his arms about her.

It was new, and yet it was familiar at the same time. He'd done this to her in her dreams. Time could stop, for all Kate cared, as long as the kiss didn't. Jake's tongue touched hers boldly, and Kate moaned. She felt his fingertips sliding with ease down the length of her spine. When his hands reached her hips, he pressed her against him. Against his hardness.

Kate pulled away suddenly, breathing hard. The dream was nice, but the realness of him frightened her.

She knew where this was leading, and she knew she'd regret it—after it was over, of course. Now she was fighting with herself. Her body wanted what she felt pressed against her. Her body wanted the reality that her mind knew in her dreams. But the last thing she wanted to have was regrets. "Stop," she said, panting. She tried to pull away from him.

"You don't want me to, Kate," he said. He didn't let her go.

She closed her eyes, trying to bring her breathing under control. "You're right." She couldn't lie to him. She knew he'd see through it. "But it's too soon. You said you wouldn't push me. You promised you wouldn't hurt me." Her lips were dry and felt swollen. Kate ran her tongue across them.

"I also said we'd handle whatever happens as it happens."

His piercing, heated gaze held hers. "I'm not ready to handle it," she said. Her throat was so dry, her words were hardly more than a whisper. Her heart was still racing from his kiss. "Please," she murmured. She knew if he didn't release her soon, there would be no denying him, no denying herself.

He let her go so suddenly, she nearly stumbled away from him. "Come on," Jake said, his voice tight. "I have something else to show you."

Off to the left of the living room was a small kitchen, with a table that extended into the living room. Jake went in the opposite direction, leading her into a bedroom. The entire length of the wall was glass there, too. The bed, which seemed too large for the room, had its headboard against the opposite wall.

"It's . . . nice," she stammered.

"I rearranged the furniture to put the bed over there. I think I did it because I knew you'd like to wake up and be able to look out over the ocean. Not to mention, it's more spacious this way."

Kate said nothing, but she did find the idea of seeing the ocean first thing in the morning appealing. She looked out again. The boat rocked gently and waves slapped against it with dull, sloshing sounds.

"What exactly do you do for a living?" Kate asked, without looking at him. Her words weren't quite steady. She was watching the waves; then her eyes moved to take in a fishing boat in the distance. She was still warm from his kiss, and she could feel his eyes on her.

"Don't you know?" he asked simply. His words were closer than she'd expected, and the warmth of his breath touched her face, spreading warmth into her body.

Kate still wasn't looking at him. She swallowed hard, working to concentrate. She should know, she thought. She rubbed her hands together nervously. "You're painting something. It's something big and bright, with many brilliant colors."

"I'm restoring the carousel down on the boardwalk," Jake put in. He turned and went back to the living room.

Kate followed. He stopped at a desk that Kate hadn't noticed before. Her thoughts had been so filled with his kiss, she'd noticed little else.

"Here's what it will look like when I'm through."

She looked down at the colorful drawings spread out before her. If the carousel turned out to look like the drawings she was seeing, it would be beautiful. Kate gazed at them for several moments in silence.

"These are beautiful." She felt touched, as though another intimate secret had passed between them. "Did you draw these as well?"

"Yes," Jake replied. He picked up several drawings of various horses. "These six are already finished. I'm doing one horse at a time. I want to make each one unique, with its own mixture of colors."

A vision of Jake Casperson standing on a scaffolding against a brick building suddenly popped into Kate's mind. The sign on the building said Little John's Used Cars—We Buy and Sell Anything. Jake was painting a bald-headed man driving an old jalopy on the side of the tall brick building. The bald man was feverishly chasing a sexy-looking girl with a big chest in a red convertible.

"You painted the mural on Little John's Used Cars," said Kate.

"Yes, that's right."

"It's located at the end of Main Street." Kate didn't even have to try to think about these things any longer. Things she couldn't possibly have known continued to pop into her mind. She wondered briefly how far this ability would go.

She'd never been to Willows Point before, and yet she now had a fairly clear idea of the entire town—all the way from the carousel at the boardwalk to the end of Main Street where Little John's Used Cars was located. Across the street from the car lot was a little Italian restaurant. Kate couldn't make out the name of it completely—Anthony's, or Antonio's, or something like that. But she could see the tables inside were covered with red-checked tablecloths, and she could almost smell the garlic.

It was enough to remind her that it was time for lunch. She turned to Jake to tell him she was hungry. But before she could even open her mouth, he said, "I'm hungry, Kate. How about Italian? I know this little place up on Main called Anthony's. I think you'll like it."

Kate looked at him with wide eyes for a moment, then she burst out laughing.

Jake smiled at her. "What's so funny?"

"This is all getting to be a little too weird. I was just thinking about that place, and I've never even seen it before. And I was about to tell you I was hungry."

Jake chuckled, but it was more at Kate's own laughter, not because he felt anything was really funny.

Kate grew serious again. "How far do you think this will go? How tuned in to each other do you think we'll become?"

Jake shrugged absently. "I haven't the slightest idea. I only know that being with you, sharing things with you, like my work, seems so right. It all feels so right." His gaze met hers. The expression in his eyes was tender. Kate knew of no other word with which to describe it. "I know that sounds corny, but it's true," Jake added, as though he were afraid she didn't believe him.

After everything Kate had experienced in her dreams and in reality the past few days, she wasn't about to not believe him. Right now, she was just about ready to believe in anything—ghosts, goblins, trolls, things that go bump in the night. It didn't matter. She was ready to believe that any sound of bells was a clear indication that Santa Claus was drawing near in his sleigh.

"So, do you want some lunch?" Jake asked.

"Yes. Will you take me to see the carousel, too?"

He reached for their coats. "Of course," he replied. He wasn't sure why, but having Kate see it suddenly seemed very important.

He took her hand. His touch, the joining of their hands, was a joining of reality with that which was not quite real. That was how it felt to Kate. She took his hand in return, took what he offered, feeling ready to face what might lie ahead for the two of them, feeling safe and warm and protected. And she understood what he meant when he said it felt right. It did, indeed, feel right. Even though that feeling was weighed down with a feeling of fear.

Anthony's turned out to be just as Kate had envisioned. The entire Main Street of Willows Point turned out to be that way. Jake took her hand again and led her into the small restaurant. He seemed to like holding her hand as much as she did. In fact, she noticed he touched her at every opportunity, from a simple nudge on the small of her back to a squeeze around her shoulders.

Kate stopped just inside the door and looked around. The small place was crowded, with few, if any, empty tables. The room was filled with politely muffled conversations. A few patrons looked at Kate and Jake for a moment before disregarding them and getting back to the meals before them.

"So you finally bring a lady to enjoy my delicious food." The man speaking approached them.

"Kate, meet Anthony. Anthony, this is Kate McCoy," said Jake.

Anthony looked as far from being Italian as he could get with his blond hair and fair skin. He was tall and lanky, his eyes the color of a bright blue sky. He took

Kate's hand and tenderly raised it to his lips. His action took Kate by surprise and caused her to blush. No man had ever kissed her hand before. She didn't think many men even did that anymore. And yet, the tingle that moved up her arm felt oddly familiar, as though she *had* been kissed on her hand before, kissed by *Anthony* before. Or at least by a man who reminded her of Anthony. She threw a quick glance to Jake to find him looking as surprised as she felt.

"And such a lovely lady, too," added Anthony.

He was looking into her eyes with such intensity that Kate felt a chill pass over her. Kate was suddenly overcome with a feeling that she was no longer standing in Anthony's restaurant. And there was a vague sound of something new. Kate thought it sounded like music. That feeling was so strong, in fact, that she quickly glanced around her, expecting to find herself in a different place.

Of course she wasn't. She was still in Anthony's restaurant, and the other patrons were still eating and ignoring them. Her eyes fell upon a jukebox back in the corner, but it was quiet.

Anthony released her hand, suddenly and with a look of surprise on his face, as though he'd been in a trance and had just snapped out of it. "I kissed your hand," he muttered.

Kate looked up at him, unblinking. "Yes." It was hardly more than a whisper.

He smiled, embarrassed. "I've never kissed a lady's hand before. But it seemed like the right thing to do when I took yours."

"Well," Jake piped, "she's with me." His voice sounded light, but Kate could sense the tightness behind it. "And, friend or no friend, the next time you kiss her anywhere, you'll have to deal with me."

As tall as Anthony was, Jake's threat seemed to pass right over his head. He offered Kate the slyest grin she'd ever seen. "I hope you'd like a booth because if you want a table near the windows, I'm afraid you'll have to wait," he said.

"A booth would be nice." That tightness was beginning to come out in Jake's voice.

If Anthony heard it, he ignored it and turned to lead them to the only empty booth. He placed two menus on the table.

Kate sat down, her face feeling warm, despite the chill that still remained in the rest of her body. Having Anthony kiss her hand and then Jake standing up to him for it made her feel as if she'd slipped into another era. The actions of both men seemed oddly out of character, and Kate wasn't quite sure how to deal with either one. She avoided looking at both men by picking up her menu.

Jake sat down across from her, and Kate could feel the burning touch of his eyes.

"Can I get you anything to drink while you're deciding which one of my delicious lunches to try?"

Kate looked up to find both men regarding her. "Could I have a cup of hot tea?" she asked. Anything warm and wet would do.

"Of course. And you, Jake?"

"I'll have the same," said Jake, never taking his eyes from Kate.

"No beer?" Anthony said. "This is a first."

Jake finally tore his gaze from Kate to look up at Anthony. "I had a few last night, and I guess they'll hold me for a while."

"Whatever you say, Jake," Anthony muttered. "I'll be back with your tea in a minute." He stepped away and went into the kitchen through a swinging door.

Kate watched him until he was gone. "He owns this place and he waits on the customers as well?" she questioned.

"No, not really. He likes to greet the customers, at least when he's not too busy. Someone else will probably bring out our orders to us," Jake explained.

"You've been friends for a long time," said Kate. She was envisioning more and more. She could see Jake as a younger man, tossing a football to a younger Anthony.

"We grew up together." He paused. "What happened when he kissed your hand?"

"I don't know," she answered honestly. "I felt that the three of us slipped into another place. I can't explain it." There was a moment of silence. "It was like the dreams. Only this time we were awake. Did you feel anything or see anything?"

"I think so," Jake replied slowly, softly.

"It was just a flash, and it involved Anthony as well," Kate noted. "And did you hear what he said about it feeling like the right thing to do? That's how everything has been feeling to us. Until now, it's just been the two of us. God, what does all of this mean?"

Anthony came out with their mugs of hot water and tea bags and set one in front of each of them just in time to hear Kate's question.

"It means it's time to order," Anthony said, smiling down at her. "Are you ready?"

Kate had looked at her menu without seeing it. "What do you suggest, Jake?"

"The cannelloni. He makes the best," Jake said shortly.

Kate forced herself to smile at Anthony. "The cannelloni it is then."

"Make it two," muttered Jake.

Anthony chuckled. "You two make this too easy. Any appetizer?" His eyes were on Kate again. "I have this great salad with my own recipe for the dressing. It's Romaine lettuce, onions, mushrooms and—"

"Lots of artichoke hearts," Kate finished.

"That's right," exclaimed Anthony. "How did you know?"

"Jake told me," she replied, looking evenly at Jake. It wasn't exactly a lie. Jake had told her through whatever type of telepathic communication they were using. "It sounds delicious. I'll try it."

"And you, Jake. And don't tell me you'll have the same."

"No, I'll have an order of your famous cheesy garlic bread," Jake said.

"Garlic bread?" Anthony piped. "How do you expect her to get close to you after eating garlic bread?"

Jake grinned. "She's going to share it with me, so we'll smell like garlic together."

Anthony laughed. Then, "I'll send someone right out with these." He headed back into the kitchen.

"It's getting stronger," Kate said softly as soon as Anthony was gone. "Isn't it?"

Jake knew what she meant. Whatever was linking them together in their dreams had crossed over into reality. The thoughts, or whatever they actually were, simply occurred.

"Yes," Jake replied finally. "And the thoughts or messages or whatever they are, are coming easier, too."

Kate dipped her tea bag up and down in her cup of hot water. "There was something else, too, when he kissed my hand."

"What?"

"Music...I think." She squeezed out her tea bag and set in on the saucer next to her spoon. "I think I heard it, but it wasn't really there. It was so quick, it couldn't have been more than one note."

"But you know there was music," Jake put in. "I heard it, too. And something else."

Kate took a sip of tea. The warm liquid trickled down her throat and warmed her insides, filling her with a calm she greatly needed. She was able to meet Jake's gaze evenly. "What?" She was almost afraid to ask, but at the same time, she needed to know.

"Colorful lights, I think. I'm not sure. Did you see anything like that?"

Kate set her cup down with a heavy thud. "I don't remember. I was thinking more of Anthony kissing my hand. No one has ever kissed my hand."

Jake grinned. "It was extremely out of character for him. He generally keeps his distance. He's a very private person whose usual contact might be a handshake. Once at a New Year's Eve party, some girl came up and kissed him at midnight, and he turned the brightest shade of red I've ever seen."

"Really?" Kate looked toward the door where Anthony had gone and smiled.

Jake nodded.

"Then that was out of character for him, wasn't it?" Kate asked. The tea and the change of course in the conversation were relaxing her. Jake, sitting across from her, relaxed her with his sense of familiarity.

Anyone watching them would have thought they had been friends for many years.

Jake glanced at the kitchen door as though he'd be able to see through the wall and look at Anthony. "Extremely. It makes me wonder..." His words faded away.

"How much it's controlling us if it's controlling Anthony, too," Kate finished for him.

"Yes," Jake replied, looking at her.

Jake had been right. Anthony didn't bring their appetizers to them. A young girl wearing a bright red apron over her sweater and jeans did, and she came out before either could say more. "Can I get anything else for you?" she asked after setting the garlic bread and the salad on the table.

"No, thanks, everything's great," Jake said as the waitress left.

Jake was cutting the loaf of garlic bread. "Do you mind if I do some work when we get to the carousel? I'm a day behind now." He had changed the subject, and Kate was glad to let him.

"Are you on a deadline?" She took a small bite of salad, watching him. He handed her a piece of bread without asking if she wanted any.

"Just my own."

"I don't mind," she finally answered his question. "Maybe I could even help you mix paint or something. Either way, I can hardly wait to see it."

Jake smiled at her from across the table. It was a slow, easy smile that reached all the way to his eyes. "And I can hardly wait to show it to you."

It was some time later when the two of them walked down the boardwalk, Jake holding Kate's hand. The sky was still cloudy, the air damp and chilly, but there was no rain. Jake's hand seemed to spread its warmth through Kate's entire body. It could have been a warm, sunny day in July with the way he made her feel.

The building that housed the carousel was large, an old, white wooden structure near the end of the walk. Kate could just imagine it in the summertime with the heavy double doors on the front slid to either side, allowing the music of the carousel to be heard down the walk.

Now, Jake slid open one door just enough for the two of them to enter. He closed it again once they were inside, and darkness fell over them for a moment until he switched on the overhead lights.

Kate gasped in astonishment at the sight before her.

The carousel was huge, a wild array of horses of various sizes, positioned in random stances. Even in its state of neglect, it was beautiful. On one side of the carousel was a big chariot pulled by four horses, with a bench seat inside for anyone who didn't want to sit upon a horse. The top of the carousel looked like a giant circus tent that had at one time been striped in green, red and white.

"It's really something," Kate said in awe.

She turned to find Jake watching her reaction intently. "It is, isn't it?" he agreed. Still holding her hand, he pulled her closer. "I plan to restore it to look even better than it did when it was first built."

Kate looked back at it. "How old is it?"

"It was put into operation in 1910."

Kate's eyes fell on the horses Jake had already painted and the one he was presently working on. His work held her spellbound.

"What do you think?" His voice broke the spell.

Kate didn't answer for a moment. She couldn't think of the words to describe what she was feeling. She tore her gaze from the horses to look at Jake. He was grinning at her.

"They're absolutely beautiful," she said softly. She reached out and touched one of the horses with a tentative finger. It was smooth and cool to her touch.

"Would you like a ride?"

Kate looked at him sharply. "Does it work?"

"Yes, the mechanical unit was redone last year. Now the guy who owns it is just waiting for me to paint it. And it needs new lights up inside the canopy. But those come last."

Kate felt a thrill pass through her as though she'd never ridden a carousel before. "Can I really ride it?" she asked, feeling like a kid again. She felt young and carefree. She felt like giggling. It was a strange sensation. And it was wonderful. She hadn't felt this happy in such a long time.

"Sure, but only if you ride on one of my horses," Jake said, stepping up onto the platform. He was still holding her hand, and he helped her up.

"Well, I wouldn't even consider riding on anything else but yours," she muttered.

"Then climb on," Jake said, his voice full of laughter. "And I'll start her up." Only then did he let go of Kate's hand. He moved to the center, pulling a switch here and turning a knob there.

Kate didn't really watch him. She climbed up on one of his horses, a beautiful black horse with a bright red saddle.

"Here goes," he called over to her.

The carousel came to life, moving in its circle. Kate's horse started its smooth ascent. Loud, happy carnival music filled the room.

And suddenly Kate was filled again with that sense of being in a different place. Only this time, it wasn't just a mere flash as it had been when Anthony kissed her hand. No, it lasted much longer.

CHAPTER SEVEN

Kaitlan nearly fell off the horse. She grabbed the vertical pole in front of her to keep from sliding off, holding it tightly enough to turn her knuckles white. The shining emerald on her finger sparkled up at her. Where had she gotten *that?* Why couldn't she remember?

She looked around her with what she knew must have been wild, frightened eyes. It was like her dreams, the dreams with Jake. But this time, she was awake. Wasn't she?

The large room was filled with people wearing strange clothes, with happy smiles on their faces. A little girl riding the horse beside Kaitlan was wearing a bright red dress with a pinafore and a ruffle around the bottom. Her tights looked thick, even thicker than the winter panty hose Kate sometimes wore.

Kaitlan turned her head slowly, trying to take in everything that was happening in an attempt to understand it. But the understanding just didn't want to come. Things seemed to be happening in slow motion. Her palms were sweating, feeling slick against the pole she gripped with all her strength. Her heart was pounding in her chest. She could feel it, she thought she could even hear it over the sound of the happy carnival music and the laughter of the crowd.

Slowly, she looked down at herself and nearly lost her grip on the pole. She was no longer wearing her coat, jeans and sweater. Kaitlan was wearing a blue-and-white-striped dress. The waist was tight, she discovered when she tried to take a much needed deep breath. And the skirt was long enough to hide her feet. The reason she'd nearly slid off the horse before was because she was no longer riding astride, but sidesaddle with both legs toward the outside of the carousel. Her hair felt different, tight on her head somehow. Kaitlan longed to reach up and feel it. But she didn't dare let go of the pole. She knew she'd fall if she did.

Her eyes moved to the crowd of people standing about the carousel. At first, the faces were only blurs. Then she was able to distinguish the features of happy people, smiling and laughing as they watched the carousel. Some were eating popcorn, others cotton candy. Some were waving or pointing.

Her eyes fell upon a man in the crowd. His gaze held hers with a lustful, knowing look. If Kaitlan's hair hadn't been pulled so tight on her head, it would now be standing up on the back of her neck as an unexplainable wave of fear washed over her. That man who watched her was like the ring on her finger. She should know him, but she couldn't place him. Her instincts knew him, and told her to be afraid of him.

The carousel moved around and the stranger was gone from her range of sight. But her fear didn't leave her. His dark eyes reminded her of some bird of prey that was preparing to swoop down upon her. She could see him again now, and he was still watching her. His eyes told her he could wait as long as he had to. But when the right time came, he'd be ready to move in....

Move in to do what? The fear in her mind cried out.

She tore her gaze from his, and her eyes fell upon someone in the crowd who was even more familiar. At least, Kaitlan thought so. It was the same face, the same height and lanky build. There was just a curly mustache where there hadn't been one before. She was almost certain. And, oh, she was indeed glad to see him.

"Anthony!" she called.

He smiled at her and waved. "Hello, Kaitlan!"

Kaitlan didn't smile back. The carousel kept moving, and Anthony was lost in the crowd. A strong wave of nausea passed through Kaitlan and she closed her eyes, wishing the carousel would stop. She was afraid she was about to lose her lunch. What had it been? Cannelloni? No, she'd eaten supper with Jacob and his parents this evening. And they'd had roast beef. She was staying the whole week with his parents. Remember?

It didn't matter what she'd eaten. If she didn't get off this carousel soon, she was going to toss her cookies. It felt more like a wild roller coaster that never stopped. The horse she was riding felt as if it were dropping a good thirty feet instead of the four or five she knew it had to be.

She passed Anthony again. He was now talking with a young woman Kaitlan didn't recognize. She intentionally avoided looking at the man with the birdlike eyes, and studied the woman next to Anthony, instead. She was wearing a hat and laughing at something Anthony had said. Then Jake walked up to stand on the other side of the man Kaitlan wanted to avoid. He was wearing a coat and a thin tie.

"Jacob!" She'd meant to call "Jake," just "Jake," but "Jacob" had come out instead.

Anthony spoke to Jacob. Kaitlan could see their lips moving. Jacob said something in return. The three men laughed. Then the other man, the one who frightened Kaitlan, said something, too. Something Jacob seemed to ignore.

Jacob blew Kaitlan a kiss. Then she was leaving him behind in the crowd.

Kaitlan had to get off.

Why was Jake out there? He was operating this wild ride, wasn't he? No, a man wearing a brown felt cap was operating it. Kaitlan remembered him now, and shifted her gaze to see him standing in the center of the carousel.

"Please," she said, "I need to get off."

No one seemed to hear her.

She closed her eyes tight. "Jake, turn it off!"

Her hands were slipping from the pole. She couldn't hold on any longer. She was sitting sideways on a saddle that wasn't made to be used that way, and she was sliding off!

The carousel stopped suddenly, and fortunately Kaitlan's horse stopped when it was in its lowest position. She slid down the side of it. Her feet touched the platform for only a moment before she stumbled to the dusty, wooden floor. She remained there in a heap, unmoving, her eyes once again closed tightly. She worked to catch her breath, feeling as though she must have held it for the entire ride, and waited for her stomach to settle.

"Kate!"

She remained motionless, relishing the blessed stillness. She never wanted to move again. She heard Jake's footsteps as he ran across the platform. Then he was on the floor beside her, grasping her shoulders so tight that she felt it through her coat and thick sweater. Panting still, she raised her eyes to meet his. And even doing that seemed to take energy she didn't possess at the moment.

"Are you all right?" He nearly yelled into her face.

Of course she wasn't all right. She would have yelled the words back at him had she had the strength. How could she be all right? She felt as if the millions and millions of cells that made up her body were trying to jump back into their rightful places all at the same time.

"I think I'm going to be sick," she muttered. Her lips were dry, her throat felt parched, and her voice was harsh, sounding more like she'd just gotten out of bed.

"Put your head between your knees," he said. With one hand on the back of her neck, he eased her head down. "And breathe deep and slow."

What did he think she was trying to do? She wanted to yell at him again. She felt as if she'd just come up after being underwater for four minutes. She heard him breathing hard, too.

She tried to draw moisture to her lips and mouth. "Did you see it?" she asked, her words sounding muffled because her face was pressed against her leg. "Did you see any of it?" If he said he didn't, she was going to ask him to take her to the nearest hospital for psychiatric evaluation.

"Yes," he replied, pulling her close to him. His arms went about her like a protective warm cover.

Well, that was a comfort. At least if she was crazy, she wasn't alone. Maybe they should go in for psychiatric evaluation together.

She raised her head and leaned against his chest. His heart beat strongly in her ear. The sound brought with it a strong sense of reality.

She looked at the carousel. It was dark and quiet now, just as it had been before, with only the horses Jake had painted looking shiny and new. It looked completely harmless, and Kate wondered why it had frightened her. But it had. It still did. She turned away from it, still shaking.

"What happened?" she asked, her voice no stronger than a whisper against him. She clung to him, relishing his stability. She felt a shiver pass through her as though someone had just opened one of those large sliding doors, and she pressed herself into him, drawing in the warmth of his body.

He kissed her brow, spreading more warmth into her with the touch of his lips. "I wish I knew. I flipped the lever and the music started. The next thing I knew, I was outside walking in."

"I saw you come in. And I just kept thinking that this couldn't be happening. But there you were standing next to Anthony and that other man. That *was* Anthony, wasn't it?" Kate's voice was hard to control, and her teeth wanted to chatter from the cold fear still swirling within her.

"Yes," Jake said softly, his breath warm against the side of Kate's face.

"How can this be happening to us, Jake? How?" she pleaded. She went on before he could answer. "I mean, this is all so impossible. People don't just suddenly find themselves in another place or another time. It just doesn't happen. Unless, of course, we've lost our sanity."

"Do you think we could lose it at the same time together?" Jake asked quietly.

"No," she replied honestly. And that in itself brought her some hope that she wasn't crazy after all. There was a moment of silence that comforted them both. They sat locked in each other's arms, needing each other as no two people had ever needed before.

For the first time, Kate was truly glad she'd come and was not facing this fear alone, this horrible, never-ending fear unlike anything she'd ever felt before. "Who was that other man?" she asked after a moment. "I should know him, too. I was afraid of him," Kate remembered. Leaning against Jake, feeling his arms around her, Kate had hoped some of the fear would lessen. But just thinking of that man brought a whole new wave of unexplainable terror, sending icy shivers up her spine. She clung to Jake even tighter.

"John," he replied. "His name was John. I knew him, too. Why were you afraid of him?"

"I don't know," she replied honestly, her words coming out slowly. "You spoke to them, to both of them."

Jake nodded, his chin lightly touching the top of her head. "Anthony asked me if I was working late—again. I said I had been."

"And that's what made you laugh?" Kate asked. "I saw you laughing." She needed to keep talking and keep listening to Jake's voice. It didn't reduce the terror she felt, but it seemed to add to her own sense of strength.

"He said, 'a man's work is never done,' and I said that when you worked for my father, it surely wasn't," Jake explained. "That made them both laugh. Then John said if I didn't stop working and keep a closer eye on my lovely fiancée', someone was bound to steal her away from me."

"Was that when you blew me a kiss?" Kate asked.

"Yes. Then the next thing I knew, you were yelling for me to turn it off and I found myself back at the lever, switching it off."

"It was so very real," Kate muttered. "Even after you switched it off, I was still sitting sidesaddle, and I just slid down the side of the horse."

Jake said nothing. He just held her.

"Jake?"

"What?"

Kate shifted slightly in his arms so she could look at the carousel again. "You painted that horse exactly as it was then."

"Oh, God," he moaned. "If that's true, do you know how long all this has been going on? Do you?" His breath came out in one fear-filled huff. And he answered his own question before Kate could. "I painted that horse first, weeks ago."

His arms tightened around her, nearing the point where Kate couldn't breathe. But she said nothing, knowing he needed to hold her just as much as she needed to be held.

Kate turned her face toward him, pressing against his chest. She didn't want to look at that carousel again. She wanted only Jake. She wanted the sure, safe feeling his arms around her gave.

The room was quiet for a long moment. There was just the soft sound of their breathing. Still pressed against Jake, Kate shifted to look up at him. Their eyes held for what seemed to be an eternity before his lips tenderly joined hers.

This time, Kate didn't fight him or pull away. Right then, she seemed to need him more than she'd ever needed anyone in her life, and he seemed to know it. She needed his touch, his feel, his realness. Whatever the two of them had just experienced, they'd experienced it together. Despite the fear, some intimate secret was drawing them together. And Jake's kissing her was just another "right" aspect of that secret. Kate understood that now. She understood it in the same sense that she knew just what his kiss was doing to her. It was bringing about a longing that Kate had long since thought was dead.

But something was wrong. Even with the heat his kiss was bringing to her, Kate still felt a dead coldness. She pulled away.

"What's the matter?" Jake asked, trying to bring his lips back to hers.

She moved out of his reach. "Not here," she whispered. "There's something cold and dark here. Something..." She didn't finish. The only word she could think of that adequately described the way she felt was *dead* and she was afraid that if she said that, Jake would really think she was crazy.

Jake wasn't feeling the same thing Kate was, and he misunderstood her words.

"You're right, it is cold here. Why don't we go somewhere warm? Do you feel steady enough to walk?" he asked.

"I think so," she lied. The fact was, between Jake's kiss and the experience on the carousel, Kate wasn't sure her legs would ever hold her again.

He helped her to her feet. She stood for a moment waiting to see if her knees buckled beneath her. Her legs were shaky, feeling more like rubber than flesh and bone. But in the end, they held her up. Jake's arm around her helped her more than anything.

Jake held her pressed against his side, his arm around her shoulders. He led her to the door.

"Where are we going?" she asked, her voice sounding much calmer than she actually felt.

"Back to Anthony's. I want to see if he was affected by this, since he was in it with us."

He slid the large door open with one hand, while he still held her with the other. As it moved, it gave a loud creak on its rusty runner.

The damp, cold air hit Kate like a splash in the face. She took a deep breath, feeling the cold air in her lungs. She felt rejuvenated; the weakness seemed to leave her just as quickly as it had come over her with the end of that experience. But she still wasn't ready for Jake to let go of her. She didn't think she'd ever be ready for that.

They walked back up the boardwalk without speaking. The only sounds were their footfalls and the usual noises of the harbor—the cries of sea gulls, the constant slapping and swishing of the ocean, the distant engine sounds of ships coming or going. The wind had picked up, stinging Kate's cheeks with its damp force, but she ignored it. She concentrated on simply taking one step at a time. Kate looked around constantly, expecting to see that the buildings and streets of Willows Point had somehow changed during her brief time on the carousel. To her great relief, things appeared just as they had before. Still, Kate shivered, feeling a cold that came from somewhere deep within her and had nothing to do with the wind that was blowing against her.

"How long did it last?" she asked. She found herself now calm enough to talk about the experience. In fact, her interest in it was almost greater than her fear. She wanted to talk about it, to learn about it. She felt drawn to it, compelled to find out all she could about it.

Their pace never faltered.

Jake gave her shoulders a gentle squeeze as though he understood her need to know. "I had my watch hand on the lever both times. It was hardly more than a minute."

"It seemed more like hours," Kate commented. Thoughtlessly, she leaned her head against the strong, muscled part of his upper arm. "And it felt more like it was moving a hundred miles an hour. I had no strength, like I was going to slide off that horse any second."

"That's how I felt, too," said Jake. "When I was walking through those doors to stand next to Anthony and John, I felt like my legs weren't going to hold me." He was holding her as close to him as he possibly could. Despite the cold, his hands were clammy, sticky almost with sweat of his lingering fear. A fear for Kate. It was a fear that he would lose her in some way.

His heart picked up its pace at the very thought. He felt as if he'd been looking for Kate all his life, and now some unknown force had led him to her. He couldn't lose her now. Even the idea of taking her back to Port James, where she would be only two hours away from him, was something he didn't want to think about.

"You didn't look like you were having trouble walking," Kate said, bringing his thoughts back in an instant.

The fresh fragrance of her hair touched him when he turned back to her again. "Nor did you look like you were going to fall off that horse," he pointed out, his voice warm against her temple.

"I didn't?" Kate asked, surprised. "I was gripping that pole so hard, my knuckles turned white."

Jake shook his head slightly, his chin brushing against her in the process. "No, you weren't. You were smiling and waving to me."

"No, I wasn't," Kate argued. "I was holding on to the pole. I remember seeing my hands. I was wearing this beautiful emerald ring."

Jake chuckled lightly. A passerby would have thought they were discussing something amusing, like a sitcom on television. "Well, that's not what I saw. You were laughing and waving. And when I blew that kiss to you, you blushed like a schoolgirl."

Kate stopped walking, forcing Jake to stop as well. She felt as though the carousel were still spinning inside her head. She'd never felt so confused in her life. "I remember when I called out to you. I was thinking 'Jake,' but 'Jacob' was what came out of my mouth." She looked at Jake intently, wishing all the answers would suddenly appear within the darkness of his eyes. She didn't even notice that rain had started falling until a large drop landed right on her nose.

Jake had no ready answers. All he knew was that the woman within the circle of his arm was at the root of everything. She was a part of him that had always been there, he just hadn't seen it until that first dream.

"Come on, let's go before it rains on us," he urged.

They walked quickly to Anthony's, without speaking again. Jake took her hand. It was easier for the two of them to move quickly through the rain that way.

They walked in, the chimes on the door ringing with their entrance.

"Back so soon?" asked Anthony. He was alone in the room, adding up a stack of receipts near the cash register.

If Kate hadn't known better, she'd have thought he looked as if he expected them. But perhaps it was just her imagination.

"So Jake has you out running in the rain, has he?" he asked before either of them could answer his first question. "You both look like you could use some coffee."

Kate and Jake sat down across from Anthony on two of the five stools in front of the small bar. "We'd like to talk to you," said Jake.

Anthony turned away. "This sounds serious." He picked up two cups near the coffeemaker. "Maybe I'd better pour myself one, too." He grabbed a third cup and poured coffee into all of them. Then he brought them around to the bar, turning away a second time to get the sugar holder and several small packets of creamer.

"So what's up, my man?" he asked Jake.

Jake muttered a thanks for the coffee as Kate put sugar in hers.

"Well, it's nothing serious, really," said Jake. "We just didn't get to talk to you much when we were here before."

Anthony looked from Jake to Kate. "What?" he asked finally. "You come all the way back up in the rain just to talk to me? Jake, you're in here nearly every week."

Kate could feel Anthony's questioning gaze on her, and she purposely kept her eyes from meeting his.

Jake shrugged off Anthony's questions. "So what's new? Anything happening around here that I've missed?"

Kate took a sip of coffee and nearly choked, thinking of her own questions: Have you had any wild, erotic dreams lately? Or have you suddenly found yourself in a different place when you thought you were in the kitchen stirring a pot of spaghetti? She forced herself to swallow and kept her mouth shut.

Anthony's brows rose in question. He glanced at Kate again. Then he laughed—hesitantly. "Jake, are you on some heavy cold medication or something?" he asked.

Jake shrugged, meeting his gaze evenly. Kate avoided looking at either of them, staring into her cup, knowing she wouldn't be able to lie so well. And she was extremely grateful Jake wasn't coming close to mentioning their dreams. "No, why?" Jake asked, never taking his eyes from Anthony's.

"I was just wondering," Anthony replied. "You're sounding and acting a little strange."

That was sure putting it mildly, Kate thought. Actually, with everything that had happened to her and Jake in the past two days, she felt they were both acting fairly normal. Well, as normal as could be expected.

"So what the hell do you want to know, Jake?" Anthony demanded.

Jake shrugged again. Kate thought he looked a little nervous about lying. "I just wondered if there was anything new happening in your life. Is that a crime?"

Yes, Kate thought, he was growing nervous. And defensive, too.

"Well to tell you the truth, Jake," Anthony said, "if there was something new happening with me, I probably wouldn't notice." And if he noticed Jake's irritation, he was polite enough to ignore it. "This is the first time in days I've had time to take care of the receipts. Every night this week, I've had to shoo the customers out at closing time. I don't remember that ever happening in the off-season before, especially when the weather is so wet and cold. You saw what it was like here at lunch. And that was light compared to the past few days."

Kate finally looked up at him and smiled. As always, it was a pleasant relief to turn to another subject—even though Kate knew it wouldn't be long before they jumped back to the dreams. "Pretty busy, huh?"

"That's the biggest understatement I ever heard," piped Anthony. "I've been staying up until the wee hours in the morning just to clean up the place for the next day. I've hardly had time to change my clothes or take a shower and shave. I'm thinking about growing a mustache just so I don't have to worry about it."

Kate stared at him, remembering the vision of him with a mustache by the carousel.

Fingering the stubble above his lip absently, Anthony smiled at her with the same expression on his face and twinkle in his eyes that he'd had when he waved to her on the carousel. Kate nearly fell off her stool. "Can you imagine me with a mustache?" he asked, his voice filled with laughter.

"Yes, I can," Kate replied without thinking. She quickly clamped her mouth shut.

"Like I said," Anthony went on, "this is the first time in several days that I haven't been swamped with customers. Not that I don't like it. Who wouldn't want more business? I just keep debating whether or not to hire another waitress and cook. I'm afraid the business will slack off as soon as I do."

Kate lifted her mug to her lips and took a sip. The coffee was strong and hot and spread warmth through her almost like one of Jake's kisses. She glanced briefly at her cup again, taking in more warmth with her hands wrapped around it. Her eyes dropped to her fingers. She nearly dropped her cup, spilling coffee down the front of her coat.

"Whoa! Kate!" cried Anthony. He quickly reached for a towel to clean up the coffee.

"What is it, Kate?" asked Jake. He moved just as quickly to take her cup and blot up what little coffee he could with a napkin.

"That ring," Kate stammered. "The ring that was on my finger left a mark." She held her hand up to Jake. "See it?" Her heart was racing again. Why was it every time she felt she was getting a grip on her fear, something had to jump out and remind her of it?

Jake looked closely at her hand and said nothing for a moment.

"What's the matter?" Anthony asked. "Did you lose a ring?"

"Something like that," Jake muttered without looking away from Kate's hand.

"Do you see it?" Kate asked again, her voice revealing the anxiety pumping through her body. Jake was holding her hand again, still looking at it. His touch was the only safe, secure thing she felt then, and she tried to draw strength from it.

"I see it," Jake replied slowly.

"What did your ring look like?" Anthony asked. Since he obviously didn't understand any of this, his voice was the only one that wasn't laced with worry.

Kate looked at him, meeting his eyes. "It was an emerald," she explained, her voice still not quite steady. "Square cut, set in gold." She remembered it with great detail. She knew that there were eight prongs holding the stone in place.

"Sounds pretty," Anthony said absently.

"It is," Kate murmured.

"It's her engagement ring," said Jake.

Both Kate and Anthony turned to him sharply.

"Engagement?" echoed Anthony.

Kate nearly echoed the same question. Why hadn't she known that before now?

"You asked her to marry you, and you never even told me?" asked Anthony. He didn't allow time for Jake to reply. "You were in here a week ago, and you never even said a word. Never even said you had a girl." He shifted and set down his mug in an angry thud on the bar.

Jake looked flustered as though he hadn't realized what he'd said until now. "I guess I wanted it to be a surprise."

"Well, it certainly was. Were you surprised, Kate?"

Kate finally tore her gaze from Jake to look at Anthony. "Oh, yes. Very," she said. She was still feeling the effects of that surprise.

"And you lost the ring on top of it. Damn, I'm sorry to hear that." Anthony was now showing greater concern. "Could you have lost it in here? I'll certainly keep an eye out for it."

"I didn't lose it here," Kate said quickly.

"Well, I sure hope you find it."

She tried to smile at him.

"Listen, folks," Anthony said, changing the subject. "You're welcome to sit here and drink as much of my coffee as you like, but I've got to get back to work. I want to get ready in case tonight turns out to be as busy as the past few nights."

"We've got to go, anyway. We'll just let you get back to work," said Jake. He took a final sip of his coffee and set down the cup. "But you know, my friend, if things keep up like this, you should consider hiring a few more people. You need more than a ten-minute coffee break."

Anthony shrugged. "A man's work is never done, you know."

Kate stared at Anthony, totally astonished. It was what Anthony had said to Jacob in the vision when Kaitlan rode the carousel.

Kate finally tore her gaze away to look at Jake. "Did you hear what he said?"

"Yes, I heard him. Come on, let's go."

"What did I say?" Anthony asked, looking at them both in wonder.

"Nothing," Jake muttered. He took Kate's arm and nearly dragged her off the stool. "Come on, Kate," he said again. "We have to go."

"Wait," Anthony called, coming out from behind the bar. "Tell me what the hell's going on with the two of you."

"We would if we could," said Jake. He pulled Kate toward the door. "We'll see you later, Anthony."

He led Kate out into the rain before Anthony could call out again.

"It is affecting him, too," Kate said.

Jake's car was still parked down the block from Anthony's restaurant, and Jake now directed her toward it. "I think you're right. And it's like he said, he's just too busy to notice it."

"Or maybe he's not getting the same signals we are," Kate put in.

Jake opened the car door for her, and Kate climbed in. Her coat was wet with rain and splotched with spilled coffee, but she didn't care. She absently wiped rain from her face. Jake climbed in and shut the door. The car was quiet for a moment, the rest of the world shut out.

"Maybe not," Jake said. "Or maybe the signals, or whatever they are, just aren't as strong for him." His hair was wet from the rain, making it look darker than it was.

"Where are we going?" Kate looked over at him. Jake took her hand and gave it a squeeze. She felt rather calm at that moment. Jake's touch always seemed to ease away her fear.

His expression was free of worry, too, and Kate thought her touch must do the same for him. Either way, she was finding she liked touching him. And she liked when he touched her. "Back to my houseboat," he replied.

"But what about your painting? I saw how much work you have to do, and I feel like I'm keeping you from it."

Jake smiled at her, and the warm brilliance of the smile washed over her, reminding her of that first time he smiled at her on her front porch. That seemed like months ago, perhaps even years, instead of just two days. "I don't think either one of us is up to seeing that carousel for a while."

Kate couldn't argue with that. She didn't think she'd ever want to get close to it again. But she still felt guilty for taking him away from his work. "But what about your work?"

"I still have the drawings at home that need work. Many of them need the detail I didn't have time to put on before," he replied. He finally started the car, releasing her hand to shift the gear into drive. "Are you afraid?" he asked. Usually, he felt her emotions so strongly. Now the signals she normally sent to him were quiet.

She shrugged. "A little, I guess. I don't really feel afraid of the actual vision we had, just confused by it. I feel more afraid that it came while we were awake."

Jake understood completely. Now that she'd said it, he realized he felt the same way.

Jake took her home to his houseboat. And the remainder of the afternoon passed slowly. He worked on his drawings while Kate checked out the small library of books he kept on a shelf in the corner of the living room. Art books made up most of his collection. She also drank more warm tea and absently watched television. Kate couldn't seem to get warm and she couldn't get the vision of the carousel ride off her mind. It kept playing through her mind with more and more detail each time, like the dreams of her and Jake.

The only thing that felt comfortable was being close to Jake. She moved around him several times and glanced at his work. She touched him in some way several times. And on the few passes when she didn't touch him, he reached out to her. Once when she leaned over to look more closely at a drawing, he absently kissed her cheek.

Outside, a storm brewed. Dark clouds gathered, and the wind whipped large waves against the boat. Somewhere in the falling darkness, a small bell clanked in the wind. Mist from the sea and moisture from the clouds mixed to form a cold, eerie fog that seemed to swallow all of Willows Point.

But inside, Kate settled on Jake's couch, finally beginning to feel warmth within her. She forced her mind to concentrate on the movie on television. The scratch of Jake's pencil as he worked on his drawings echoed through the room, bringing a feeling of coziness to Kate, of home, of something familiar. She liked the idea that he was close. She liked being with him on his houseboat. And she didn't even realize she'd dozed off. Until the dream started....

CHAPTER EIGHT

Again, there was music. But Kaitlan wasn't on the carousel this time. She was dancing. And the music came from a live orchestra.

Still wearing the striped dress, a dress that swayed and flowed, Kaitlan danced inside a large, round, open pavilion to the music of a waltz.

For a moment, she nearly stumbled. But her partner was an expert dancer and managed to keep the two of them circling around with hardly a break in their step. As a matter of fact, he held her unusually tight.

Kaitlan stared up at the man who held her. His hair was as dark as his coat. He was tall and smiled down at her. It was a smile that never reached his eyes. She recognized him. He was John, the man who'd teased Jacob that someone would steal her away from him. That same unexplainable wave of fear washed over her, nearly taking her breath away. She knew there was something she should remember about him, but couldn't.

"I dance rather well, don't you agree?" he asked. "And it's a good thing, too, Kaitlan, darling. I'd thought you might have crippled me before."

His words made little sense to Kaitlan.

Several details of the night touched Kaitlan instantly. It was a clear night lit by a moon and millions of twinkling stars in the sky. Music and laughter filled the air, as they had in her vision of riding the carousel. The pavilion was as crowded as the carousel had been. There were young couples walking arm in arm. There were old people. There were entire families.

John pressed her against the hardness of his thighs suddenly, bringing her immediate, total attention to him. She felt heated color rise up her neck to her face.

"Please don't do that," she said, trying to speak loudly enough over the music that he could hear her without drawing any attention.

John glanced around absently. "Why not? Jacob's not around to see. He's off arguing with his father about running the company, as usual. What's wrong with a little fun? I know you want it."

Kaitlan felt her own eyes widen at his boldness. "I do not!" She tried to pull out of his arms then, but he refused to let her go.

"Of course you do," he insisted. "You can't tell me those little looks you give me all the time mean nothing."

"What looks? I don't know what you're talking about," she said honestly. She was rigid in his arms.

His smile never wavered. "Be honest with me now, Katie, darling. You're only marrying Krinshaw for his money, right? And it's me you love. It's me you want."

"That's absurd." She was pulling away from him with every ounce of strength she possessed, and still she was no match for him. The music went on, and no one gave them a second glance.

They danced near the steps leading down from the pavilion, and with the grace of a panther, John led her down them. It was such a smooth move, Kaitlan hardly realized they'd stopped dancing until her feet touched the grass. Just as quickly, he had her arm linked tightly within his.

"Come with me, Kaitlan," he ordered through a tight smile. "Or you'll experience the greatest humiliation of your life."

Kaitlan didn't care. All she cared about was escaping him. Her senses warned her that he was indeed a dangerous man. And she had to get away from him. She had to get to Jacob, no matter how much humiliation she experienced. She remembered suddenly why she was so afraid of John. He had tried to hurt her before. She had to tell Jacob. She had to let Jacob know just how dangerous John was.

"Let me go or I'll scream!" she said. There was no way she could let him take her away from the crowd.

"It will be the last sound you ever make, my love," he replied calmly. There was, however, nothing calm in the look in his eyes or the way he held her arm. She felt the sudden poke of something sharp against her side and knew instantly it was the blade of a knife. It was suddenly hard to breathe. Fear touched her deep within, and it seemed to radiate a sick, hot feeling throughout her entire body. She'd never been so frightened. Her hand was numb, and she felt that if he squeezed any tighter, her bones might snap in two.

John's eyes were alive with dark, lusty fire that showed his want of her so boldly that Kaitlan shivered despite the heat of the summer night. He smiled down at her, and Kaitlan expected to see fangs instead of his teeth.

"Where are you taking me?" she demanded.

They drew near the edge of the park. The crowd was thinning. She felt the blade of his knife touch her with every step.

"I have something to show you," he replied curtly, pulling her along without slowing.

He led her away, through the emptying streets. Anyone they passed appeared to be making his way quickly to that celebration in the park, and paid them no attention. After only a few blocks, buildings grew scarce, and Kaitlan knew what was in the direction they moved. It was the ocean. They were heading toward the shore, toward the rocky cliffs.

Now there were no people at all about them. There were no longer any buildings or houses, and they had only the light of the moon.

"I want to go back. You're insane. Let me go!" she pleaded. She'd never once stopped trying to find a way to escape him. But it was a useless effort. "Jacob will be looking for me."

Her heart was pounding in her chest with fear, and a small voice was speaking inside her, saying, You fool, why were you stupid enough to let him bring you out here alone? Now there's no one to help you. No one at all.

"And by the time he finds you, it will be too late, my darling. You'll already belong to me. In body and soul." John spoke without even looking at her. He simply looked ahead, holding her tightly and pulling her along. "I tried to warn him that someone would steal you away from him, but he wouldn't listen. And of course, he was too blind to see that I would be the one to do the stealing."

Fear ripped through her like one of the waves breaking against the rocks. "No." It was hardly more than a harsh whisper. Her voice was too tight to speak. She fought harder and screamed, fearing him more than the knife. "No!"

They were almost to the cliff. Kaitlan was pulling away and kicking at him. She cursed her skirts for getting in the way. "No! No!" she cried over and over. "If you do this, Jacob will kill you."

John finally stopped pulling and turned her to face him. He touched the blade of the knife to her cheek, quieting her instantly. He only laughed in her face. "Perhaps if he's lucky or quick enough. Not that it matters. All that matters is having you. Being inside you. I don't think he'll want you anymore after that, since you won't be as pure as he thinks you to be. He'll know that every time he takes you, you'll be comparing him to me." He used the knife to cut off the top button of her dress.

Kaitlan spit in his face.

Just as fast, he released her and slapped her. His open hand whistled across her cheek with enough force that her head snapped to one side. She nearly lost her balance completely and would have fallen had he not taken her arm again, keeping her rooted to the spot.

The slap didn't stop Kaitlan, though. As soon as she regained her balance, she tried to bite his arm. But he seemed to like it. To her amazement, he put the knife away and pulled his arm from her teeth. He smiled. "Oh, Katie, I'm going to enjoy taming you." Then he hit her again, hard enough to nearly knock her off her feet.

He shifted his hold on her, sliding his closed hand down her arm. Before Kaitlan even understood what he meant to do, he pried the beautiful emerald ring from her finger. His action was swift enough to tear the flesh from her knuckle as well. "I don't think you'll be needing this any longer, sweet Kaitlan," he ground out.

"No, please, John," she begged, reaching for his closed fist that held the ring.

He shoved her to the ground and covered her with his body before she had the chance to slither away from him. She screamed once, but the scream was cut off when he covered her mouth with his rough, demanding lips. She tried to turn her head and found it impossible. So she grabbed on to his lip with her teeth and bit as hard as she could, refusing to let it go. She tasted the bitter taste of his blood, and heard him cry out at the same time.

He pulled away, and Kaitlan felt the moist flesh of his lip tear within her grasp. She smiled at him, feeling the coolness of the air touching the warmth of his blood on her mouth. But her satisfaction was short-lived for his closed fist came crashing into the side of her face hard enough that everything went black momentarily. And when she did begin to focus again, she saw stars.

Then the weight of him was gone suddenly and could have been lifted off by some unknown sea god as far as Kaitlan was concerned. There was a new voice, a voice she knew instantly, the voice of the man who had read poetry to her just two days before. Jacob's voice.

"How dare you touch her? I'll kill you for this, Tallon!" Jacob's voice came to her from far away, but there was no mistaking the hardness of it or the angry hatred in it.

Kaitlan blinked several times, focusing just in time to see Jacob's fist meet with John's jaw. That collision made a strange sound, like a *thunk,* that was instantly swallowed by the roar of the sea crashing against the nearby rocks. The blow sent John stumbling away where he tripped over Kaitlan's legs. He pulled himself up without any hesitation, absently wiping the new blood that oozed from another cut on his lip.

"He has a knife," Kaitlan warned as John pulled it out.

Just as fast, Jacob kicked it from his hand. "You can't seem to fight fair, can you?" Jacob muttered.

Dizzy though she was, Kaitlan dragged herself to her feet. On shaking legs, she stepped back from the men, who now eyed each other squarely.

The fight was on. Both men were nearly the same size, and the struggle remained even for several blows. One would hit the other, then he would strike back. It went on and on this way. One would fall, and the other would hardly get a kick in before the downed man would get up and start the fight again.

Jacob took a sudden hard punch that knocked him on his back. Kaitlan screamed.

John delivered a kick to Jacob's ribs. Jacob rolled with the blow, but John punched him again and again before Jacob could get his bearings. Kaitlan didn't realize the cliff was so close until suddenly John pushed Jacob over the edge.

Kaitlan screamed again, filling the night with a bloodcurdling cry. She was on her feet and running to the edge. But when she looked over, there was no sign of Jacob. He'd already been swallowed by the darkness of the raging sea. Pain ripped through her. She felt her heart had suddenly been wrenched from her body and torn into hundreds of tiny shreds.

She hurled herself at John so hard that she drove him backward a few steps. "You bastard!" she screamed over and over. Her vengeance gave her strength, and she used all she had against him, kicking, biting, scratching, jabbing at him with her small fists. "You'll hang for this!" She was screaming hysterically. Tears were streaming down her cheeks.

She wasn't actually hurting him, because of her small size. Still, in frustration, John shoved her away, throwing her over the cliff.

As she went over, she clutched for something to keep her from falling. Her hands only touched air. Then there was nothing under her. She was falling into nothingness, the sounds of the sea loud in her ears. She followed Jacob, her one true love.

Kate rolled off the couch. She cried out, clutching at the large rug on the floor. Her heart was beating so fast and so strong, she thought it must be trying to escape from her chest. She couldn't breathe, her lungs feeling as if they might explode at any second. Darkness engulfed her, and she knew it was the sea, trying to steal the life from her, trying to drag her down and keep her for its own. She couldn't hold her breath any longer. She inhaled, expecting to feel the burning of the water in her nose. But she woke with a start when oxygen entered her lungs.

She had no idea how long she remained on the floor, panting, looking up at the ceiling until it finally came to her where she was. Then everything seemed to touch her at once. The dream, as well as the reality that she was still on Jake's houseboat.

Where was Jake?

She tried to get up and found she didn't have the strength. She grew dizzy, and the room spun when she sat up.

"Jake?"

There was no answer. She could see the desk from where she sat. The chair was empty. The pencil Jake had been using rested in the middle of his drawing. She crawled on her hands and knees around the end of the couch, and nearly bumped into him.

He was on the floor, unconscious.

"Jake!" Kate slapped his face to wake him. But her slap merely forced his head to face away from her. "Jake, wake up!"

She lifted one muscular arm and shook it. She got no response. Panic filled her, and she felt her heartbeat race again. She placed her hand on his nose for a moment. "You're not breathing!" Fear knotted suddenly inside her. She threw herself over him, placing her ear on his chest. She heard his heart beating, much weaker than she'd heard it before when he'd held her close. "Thank God," she muttered.

But there was still the fact that he wasn't breathing. She had to get him to breathe. As a teacher, she was trained to cope with such emergencies. She was thankful, too, for her instinct, for it was instinct that took over. Kate's panic and fear for Jake were simply too strong for her to think rationally. She started artificial respiration, holding his nose and blowing her own life's air into his body. All the time, her own heart was pounding in her ears like a bass drum.

She watched his chest rise and fall and muttered a soft, "Come on, Jake. Come back to me."

With her second breath, Jake came back—coughing and sputtering as though he'd really been underwater. Kate took his hand and said nothing while he worked to catch his breath. Silently, she said a prayer of thanks.

Jake pulled himself up to sit next to Kate. "That son of a—" he started. "I think he broke my nose. I thought he'd nearly taken my head off." He lightly touched his nose with two fingers, only to find blood when he took them away.

Kate gasped at the sight of the blood. Jake pulled out a handkerchief and held it to his nose.

"I'll get you some ice." She jumped up, then had to stop again for a moment to allow another wave of dizziness to pass. She grabbed a few cubes from his freezer and wrapped them in a paper towel. She brought them to him and placed them gently on his nose. "Lean your head back," she instructed.

He leaned his head back against her, and Kate held him with one arm while she held the ice with the other.

"Were you asleep, Kate?"

"Yes. Were you?"

"No." He closed his eyes for a brief moment. "One minute, I was drawing the horse. The next thing I know, I'm walking up the hill toward the lighthouse near the cliffs."

His head rested in Kate's lap, and she found she liked holding him. She liked it a lot. She tried to concentrate on the feeling of him against her in order to push out the fear she still felt from that last experience. But the fear remained, rippling through her like a stream. "And then what?" she asked. Dream or no dream, she resisted the urge to lean down and touch her lips to his. That urge seemed to be the only thing that matched her fear in intensity.

"I heard a scream. I knew it was you, and I started running. When I saw him on top of you—" He stopped and drew in a long breath. "I felt like strangling him right then and there, but I figured he deserved a fair fight, even though he never offered the same to you." Jake paused, and a bitter laugh escaped him. "It just seemed like the gentlemanly thing to do at the time."

"But it wasn't me," Kate persisted. "Not really. I mean, you don't really think we traveled through time, do you? We couldn't have. It's impossible."

"Hell if I know," Jake muttered. "I do know that my nose feels like it's broken and this is real blood coming out of it. And if I ever see that guy standing on a street corner, I think I just might push him out in front of a taxi." He also knew he liked the feel of her holding him, his head pushed against her breast. He could smell her strong, womanly fragrance and her hint of perfume. He liked that, too, and he knew he had no desire whatsoever to move away from her.

"Maybe you hit it when you fell off your chair," Kate suggested with high hope. At this point, she was ready to believe almost anything if it would take away her unending terror. As if the vision itself hadn't been enough, there'd been finding Jake so near death. Her heart picked up pace just thinking about it.

"And just why did I fall off my chair?" he returned. "I was wide-awake. And why did you give me mouth-to-mouth resuscitation?"

"You weren't breathing." It was a simple answer to a simple question, and Kate felt foolish saying it.

"And why wasn't I breathing, Kate?" he asked sarcastically, looking up at her, his brown gaze darkening as it held hers. "Because I was underwater, that's why," he answered his own question.

Kate shook her head. This was becoming too real, too frightening, and she didn't know if she could deal with the fear. "It has to have been a dream. And you know how people say if you fall or have a heart attack in a dream, you can die. Well, it's simple, you were dreaming you were underwater and you stopped breathing."

"I was *never* asleep!" he persisted, his voice hardening. "Just like neither of us were asleep when you rode that carousel."

Kate sighed heavily, feeling a whole new wave of fear wash through her. Each wave seemed bigger than the last. Instinctively, she tightened her hold on Jake's shoulder. "Jake, we were not there," she said in a low voice, her words coming out slowly. "We could not have been there."

"Then how do you explain this?"

"I don't know!" she yelled at him, her voice filled with denying anger. She relished in the strong feeling of anger. It was so much easier to handle than the fear.

"Then how can you be so sure we weren't there?" Jake had an equal amount of anger in his voice.

"Because if we'd really been there, then we'd both be dead, because he shoved us both over the edge."

"He pushed you over, too?" Jake's voice lowered, his eyes narrowed, and something passed over his expression. Something that Kate would have classified as cold, sharp hatred.

"Yes," she replied. "I woke up before I hit the water because I rolled off the couch. I mean, I woke up before the other Kaitlan hit the water."

"That bastard!" Jake said it with such vengeance that if Kate hadn't known better, she'd have thought John really *had* pushed her and Jake over the cliff.

"Jake, we are *not* dead. This really didn't happen to us. It happened to someone else and it was just a dream, pure and simple." She tried to convince him, while trying to convince herself, as well. "Can't you see that?"

Jake took her hand and lifted the ice from his nose. "Sure," he replied, his voice filled with sarcasm. "I can also see that if you hadn't given me mouth-to-mouth, I might be dead now."

Kate opened her mouth to reply, and Jake interrupted her. "I can also see that we, you and I, somehow became those two people who died. I don't have any idea as to the how, but I think I'm beginning to understand the why."

"I don't want any more of this, Jake. I've had enough," Kate said, turning away from him, trying to turn away from the whole ordeal. She slipped out from under him, and Jake had to catch himself and sit up in order to keep from hitting his head on the floor.

"I mean this is really crazy," Kate went on, her voice laced with a touch of oncoming hysteria. "These are just dreams. And dreams do not govern a person's life. They don't take over. They're supposed to fade away with the night." She pulled herself to her feet, ignoring the lingering dizziness. Jake followed suit, still holding the ice on his nose.

"So, Kate, why are they here taking hold of us while we're awake?"

Kate wasn't looking at him, she was looking around the room. "I don't know and I don't care," she said, her voice sounding as if she really didn't.

"What are you looking for?"

"My coat," she replied absently. "Where did I leave it? There it is."

He set the ice on the nearby counter, grabbed her and pulled her close before she had the chance to reach for it. "Kate," he said softly.

"Let me go, Jake," she said, trying to ignore the way the sound of his voice sent a tingle up her back. The last thing she needed was his touch. Her fear was nearly driving her mad, drawing her to anything that might bring some comfort. And right then, it was Jake she was being drawn to. It was Jake who could give her the comfort she needed, make her forget the fear.

"No," Jake said, even softer. The warmth of his word touched her ear like velvet. "I can't let you go."

"Why not?" She felt like crying suddenly. And she finally gave up fighting to escape his arms.

He held her closer when he felt she was no longer resisting, and he pressed his face against her neck where he could inhale the soft scent of her. "Because I think we have to stay together so we can help them."

"Help them?" she echoed. "How can we help them? They're already dead!" Her voice rose again slightly.

"I don't know, it's just a feeling I have." He also had the feeling that he simply didn't want to let her go.

"Besides," Kate pushed on, hoping for a logical answer, "judging by the style of my clothes and those of everyone around us in the dreams—or whatever they are—this has to have happened nearly a hundred years ago."

"It was 1911," said Jake.

"How do you know that?" Kate eyed him with disbelief. His eyes looked darker again.

"There was a banner stretched across the entrance to the park. Didn't you see it?"

Kate thought for a long moment. Then she shook her head. She'd been concentrating on John, and where he was trying to take her. She had paid little attention to anything else.

"It said Welcome to Willows Point's Independence Day Celebration, 1911."

"I never saw it," Kate muttered. "Because *I* didn't pass under it. Some other Kaitlan did. Not me."

"Well, I did," Jake snapped. "*We* did. It was red, white and blue. We passed right under it when we entered the park after you rode the carousel."

Kate blinked in surprise. "I thought you said when the vision started for you when you were walking toward the cliff?"

"I did, didn't I," he replied slowly. "The rest is just like a memory, like the way I knew all those things about you. You and I walked from the carousel to the park in the village square. We walked, arm in arm, under that banner. Anthony and his girlfriend, Marilee, were with us. The park was crowded and lit with lamps. We danced in the pavilion. John asked to cut in just as I saw my father and—"

"And you said you needed to tell him something," Kate finished, suddenly remembering, too. "I wanted to go with you—I mean, Kaitlan wanted to, but it happened so fast—"

"God!" Jake let out a huff. "Why did I leave you there with him! You didn't want to dance with him. I remember you wanted to stay with me. You had this pleading look in your eyes. It happened so fast. And I thought I'd only be gone a minute." He swore again.

Kate shook her head once more. She didn't really remember why she hadn't wanted to dance with John. But right then, she did not think it really mattered. "*You* didn't leave *me* with him. Jacob Krinshaw left his fiancée, Kaitlan, with him."

"Krinshaw..." Jake muttered. "That was my—I mean his name, wasn't it?"

"It was what John called you—I mean him. The other Jacob," she put in, her voice still high with anger.

"But don't you see they are linked to us somehow? Or maybe we became them."

"No!" Kate argued. They were now standing face-to-face, close together. "Dead people cannot be linked to live people!" she insisted. A new wave of fear rippled through her at the thought.

"I don't believe that's true," he said simply.

"Well, I do," she shot back.

"Because if it were true, they wouldn't be leading us to them, would they!"

"If it were true, it would give them the power to be able to kill us, right?" Her fear was growing, sending shivers up her spine with each new realization.

"My God, Kate!" he exclaimed suddenly, his expression softening. "What the hell happened to your hand?"

Kate had been so busy worrying about Jake and his nosebleed and the direction their conversation was taking, she hadn't noticed her own hand, hadn't even noticed the pain. She looked down and gasped at the drying blood on the third finger of her left hand.

"He tore off my ring," she said slowly, her voice no more than a whisper. "I mean he tore *her* ring off." She simply refused to believe this wasn't happening to someone else. And still, the terror that passed through her as she looked at her finger nearly took her breath away and gave her a feeling of light-headedness.

Kate couldn't tear her gaze away from her finger. The flesh of her knuckle was cut from the harsh, quick removal of a ring. There was dried blood streaked down her hand. She slowly closed her hand, making a fist. Her knuckle felt tight. She looked at her hand as though it weren't really her hand she was seeing.

She closed her eyes. This had to be a dream, she pleaded mentally. This had to be a nightmare. She hoped that when she opened her eyes again, she'd find it really was all a dream. But she opened her eyes to see Jake, and she knew it wasn't just a dream, it was a nightmare. "I could have bumped it on something when I rolled off the couch," she said slowly, her voice filled with hope.

"Kate," Jake said softly. Any other time, Kate would have thought his voice was seductive.

He took her in his arms again. She was limp against him, and he didn't like the faraway look in her eyes.

"Take me home, Jake, please," she said softly against him. She felt tired, as though the fear had somehow taken all her energy. "I don't want any more of this. I want to go home and sleep until Monday morning. I don't want to feel any more of this fear. I don't want to feel anything."

"I can't, Kate," he said simply, giving her the comfort of his arms and the closeness of his body, because it was all he could offer her then. "I have to keep you with me. We have to see this through—together."

"You promised," she reminded him, her voice harsh, her throat tight with building fear.

"I can't," he said again, tightening his hold on her when she tried to pull away from him. The thought of her falling asleep and not being able to wake up frightened him more than the dreams did. What would have happened had she not awakened in time to give him mouth-to-mouth? Would she have stopped breathing, too, because the vision had taken her into the sea as it had him? Would they both have been found dead later, having been deprived of oxygen for some unknown reason? The thought made him shudder.

She pulled herself away with all her strength and managed to put some distance between them. "Then I'll find my own way home. And don't expect me to ever believe your promises again, Jake," she snapped.

He reached for her and she slipped away. "You can't leave."

"You can't stop me." She moved to the door without her coat.

She had her hand on the knob when he managed to wrap his arms about her waist and drag her up against him. "Kate, I can't let you leave. We have to stay together. We have to watch out for each other, don't you see that?"

She fought his hold on her for a few seconds. Then she was quiet for a long moment. "We have to make sure that we both wake up after these—these episodes. Don't we?" she said slowly, her voice still telling him she didn't want to believe it.

"I think so," he said softly, trying to ignore the way she was pressed up against the front of him.

She gave in and relaxed against him. The room was quiet.

Jake felt as if she'd died in his arms. All the fight was gone from her; she was limp against him. He looked down at her, knowing he had to do something to bring her back to him, to make her feel alive. He had to show her she couldn't give up, not now. Neither of them could. From those first dreams, he knew the one true thing that brought them both to life in more ways than one. He turned her around to face him. And he leaned down to start it.

With a gentle touch of his lips on hers.

CHAPTER NINE

The touch was simple. Easy. Precise. Gentle.

Kate's world exploded at the contact. Everything around her came to a crashing halt, except for the tingling of excitement racing through her veins. Even if she'd had the strength to fight the sudden rush of desire pulsing through her, she didn't have the will. And she realized she'd probably never have the will to fight off the sensation of Jake's lips.

Jake's lips grew urgent, hungry. And Kate moved right along with him, allowing the velvet caress of his lips to move throughout her body like a slow flame. As one kiss ended, another began. Their rhythm matched the even beating of her heart.

Jake eased her down until she was lying on the floor. The weight of him was comfortably distributed on her, his hardness pressing against her. His familiar, masculine aroma filled her and woke her senses just as the touch of his lips did. It was like a drink of wine, making her slightly dizzy again.

Her body came to life with the rest of her senses, responding in a way she couldn't have controlled even if she'd wanted to. It snapped her out of the feeling of despair she'd had only a few minutes before. Her breasts were suddenly hard, pushing against his chest. Her clothes were suddenly too tight, and her hips ground against him.

Jake pulled away slightly. "Slow down, honey," he whispered. He returned his lips to hers for a moment before moving down her throat.

Kate turned her head to give him easy access to her neck. She didn't want to slow down. She knew from the dreams—if they were indeed dreams—just how he could make her feel, and she was eager to feel that way now. Her body was crying out for his touch.

As though he heard those cries, Jake's hand snaked under her sweater to cup her breast. He turned her slightly and unhooked her bra. Then he moved the lacy hindrance out of the way as his heated touch met her soft flesh.

Kate groaned at his touch and arched against him, her breast filling his hand.

"Nice..." he murmured into her ear. He played with her nipple, feeling the way it turned hard between his fingers. Then he went on to explore every aspect of her before doing the same to the other breast.

Kate was nearly wild with want. Her body felt as if it were on fire. It had to be with the heat she felt pouring out of her. Her insides were quivering and shaking in different directions, as if tiny bolts of lightning were striking all throughout her body, each one touching down in the pit of her stomach. She couldn't remember ever having felt like this. Ever. Except in the dreams.

"Oh, Jake! Please," she begged.

Jake chuckled, the throaty sound only adding to the heat she already felt.

"Please, Jake." She was pushing her hips against his, feeling him, needing him.

"No, love, you're not nearly ready."

Kate almost screamed. Not ready? She'd never felt more ready in her life.

Seeming to read her mind, he went on. "Not until I've tasted and explored every single inch of you."

Kate groaned at that, knowing she'd never make it that long. She'd burn up first.

Jake read her mind again. "You'll make it just fine. And when you do, you'll find it's even better than the dreams."

With hands that moved ever so slowly, ever so gently, he finished undressing her. His hands and fingers spread over her at every opportunity. He helped her sit up before him and slip her sweater over her head. His hands traced up her stomach over both breasts as he slowly moved the sweater up. And everywhere he touched her, he left her skin tingling and burning. It was like a slow, exotic striptease, only Jake was doing the undressing for her. When Kate's hands moved to the snap of her jeans, he took them and moved them away again. "Let me," he said softly.

Fine, she thought. But tit for tat. If he could drive her nearly insane with his touch, with this waiting, she could do the same for him. And she went about doing just that, moving her hands to unbutton his shirt. His flesh shivered beneath her fingertips, and Kate smiled, liking the way her touch had the same effect on him as his had on her.

They took turns after that. Jake would slowly take off a piece of Kate's clothing, touching all the flesh that was exposed with its removal. Then Kate would do the same to Jake.

Minutes turned to hours. Jake touched her everywhere, and Kate did the same to him. He made love to her while never actually joining their bodies. His lips

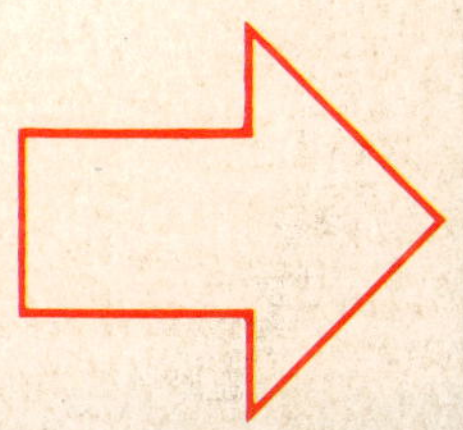

NO COST! NO OBLIGATION TO BUY!
NO PURCHASE NECESSARY!

PLAY "LUCKY 7"
AND GET AS MANY AS FIVE FREE GIFTS . . .

HOW TO PLAY:

1. With a coin, carefully scratch off the silver box at the right. This makes you eligible to receive two or more free books, and possibly another gift, depending on what is revealed beneath the scratch-off area.
2. Send back this card and you'll receive brand-new Silhouette Shadows™ novels. These books have a cover price of $3.50 each, but they are yours to keep absolutely free.
3. There's no catch. You're under no obligation to buy anything. We charge nothing—ZERO—for your first shipment. And you don't have to make any minimum number of purchases—not even one!
4. The fact is thousands of readers enjoy receiving books by mail from the Silhouette Reader Service™ months before they're available in stores. They like the convenience of home delivery and they love our discount prices!
5. We hope that after receiving your free books you'll want to remain a subscriber. But the choice is yours—to continue or cancel, anytime at all! So why not take us up on our invitation, with no risk of any kind. You'll be glad you did!

made love to her. His touch made love to her. His hands made love to her. Every inch of her body was quivering from it.

"If you don't stop and make love to me, Jake, I'm going to run up the dock and find someone else who will." Kate's voice quivered and she sounded slightly out of breath.

Kate was on the floor, facedown, her cheek pressed against the rug. Jake had just finished removing her socks, and he was kissing the back of one of her calves while his hands massaged the rest of her leg. One hand snaked up the inside of her thigh while the other moved to her foot.

It was a long moment before Jake replied, and Kate thought that he must not have heard her. Then he moved, with the gracefulness of a cat, placing the length of his body on her, against her back. "No, you won't." His harsh, warm whisper touched her cheek. "I could no sooner cut off my own hand than let you go, Kate."

Those words sounded oddly familiar, but all coherent thought had long ago slipped from Kate's mind. She had no idea where she'd heard them before. They were lost to her then, for Jake leaned over to suck gently on her neck. His lips started a whole new fire there.

"Jake, please," she begged. Her eyes were closed, her body was nearly shaking, seeking release.

He moved off her, and Kate lay waiting to feel his next move. When she felt nothing, she opened her eyes to find him reaching into his wallet. She closed her eyes again and listened to her own heartbeat pounding in her ears. It raced, with no indication of slowing.

"Turn over, Kate," he ordered, his voice harsh with desire.

Kate needed no more ordering. "It's about time," she muttered, once again facing him. Her whole being was filled with anticipation. It was hard to believe he could make her feel any better than he already had. Yet she knew the feel of him from the dreams. She knew what was coming.

And when he finally did come to her, joining them together in body and soul, it was as he'd said. It was better than the dreams.

After, Kate slept there on the floor for some time, wrapped in the warmth of him. Jake didn't sleep, though. He was too busy watching her sleep and remembering the feel of her. He tried to carry her to his bed, but his movements awakened her. And the two of them only made it as far as the floor just inside his bedroom. He couldn't seem to get enough of her. It was as though he'd been starving for her all his life, and now that he had her, he couldn't seem to get enough. And with the way she was responding, he knew she must be feeling the same way.

"How about a shower?" he whispered softly. "It will give me the chance to rub soap all over you."

"That sounds wonderful," she murmured through the darkness to him. She found his lips then without any problem. But it took them a little longer to reach his bathroom. They stayed in the shower until the hot water was used up. He dried her gently with a large, fluffy towel while she dried him at the same time, their bodies touching as the towels rubbed them.

They finally reached his bed some time near dawn. Both of them slept then, overtaken by sheer exhaustion. And for the first time in the past several days, their sleep was peaceful and unbroken.

Jake woke first just before noon. He lay still for a while listening to Kate's breathing. There seemed to be no space between them, their limbs entangled in such a way that they seemed to be locked together, as close as possible.

He gently moved her, trying to slide out of bed without waking her. His movement brought a murmured sigh from her that sounded oddly filled with disappointment. But she did not awaken.

Giving his nakedness little thought, he silently walked into the living room. Looking at the rug, he thought of Kate and their time together. It was nearly enough to make him turn around and head back into the bedroom to wake her. But the drawing of the carousel horse on his desk drew his attention. He looked at it closely, feeling there was something he should know about it, some memory he should have, something it was trying to tell him or remind him. But no matter how hard he looked at it, nothing came to him.

Only a chill that passed right through him, causing him to shiver. He crossed his arms, ignoring it, pushing himself to concentrate on the drawing.

Drawing, sketching, painting had always been a part of Jake's life. From the time he was a child with his first box of crayons, he'd shown great promise. And his talent in the world of art had never let him down.

He had studied several different carousels before taking on this job. He wanted this one to reflect the time period from which it had come, and he wanted it to hold its own grandeur for the present. He'd spent endless hours in the Willows Point Public Library studying and sketching and thinking.

The thought grabbed him suddenly like a large hand wrapped around his middle. The library. Why hadn't he thought to go there before now? The Willows Point Historical Society housed its archives there. All the village's old newspapers, photographs, papers, clothing, paintings—everything was stored in the basement of the library building.

He turned back to the bedroom to wake Kate, but one look at her peaceful expression stopped him. He knew that since the beginning of the dreams she'd had very little peaceful sleep. He decided to leave her. She looked so sound asleep, he'd probably be back before she even woke. And then if he found anything, he could share it with her. He studied her sleeping form another moment, smiling, thinking of the way she was bound to be upset that he left her sleeping. His smile grew as he thought of ways he would want to appease that anger.

He scribbled her a quick note.

> Gone to the library. Be back in time to fix breakfast for you. (I mean lunch!)

He left it on the pillow beside her and softly kissed her cheek, drawing another sleepy murmur from her. He looked at her a moment longer, embedding her beautiful, peaceful expression in his memory. Then he quietly left.

There was no more rain, and the sun was doing its best to show through the clouds. The winds were calmer, and the day felt noticeably warmer than the day before.

An hour later found him at the library. He'd stopped at Marilyn Chambers's house on the way. She was the librarian and a friend who'd helped him research the carousel, and she'd come with him to let him in.

Jake sat in front of the microfilm projector, flipping through the Willows Point *Times* for July 1911. Marilyn had promised him one hour, and he was paging through the newspapers as fast as he dared. As yet, he hadn't once even seen the name of Krinshaw.

He paused and closed his eyes. When he opened them, he watched Marilyn for a moment beyond the screen. She was putting away children's books. The way she moved reminded him of...

"Oh, God," he muttered softly. She was Marilee, the woman who had been with Anthony in the vision at the carousel.

How far did this thing go? he wondered. Absently, he rubbed the bridge of his nose and tried to push the wondering thoughts from his mind. He didn't have time now. His hour was passing.

But now he thought of Kate at home in his bed. He would have thought that after the night they'd spent together, he'd be the one exhausted. But the strange thing was, he wasn't the least bit tired. He felt a need to be here at the library, reading old newspapers. He felt his heart actually contract with a beat thinking about Kate, wishing she were there with him now just so he could hold her hand or kiss her cheek. Oh, well, he'd hurry and find whatever there was to find, then he'd hurry home to kiss her whole body. The thought made him smile.

He looked back at the screen and flipped to the next week's paper, his frustration mounting. It showed in his expression as well. He moved through the weekly Willows Point *Times* of September 1911. And there was still nothing. Not even an article concerning anyone missing.

"What the hell?" he muttered. He knew everything that had happened. He knew it was much more than any dream, but he couldn't find a single sentence regarding Jacob Krinshaw or his fiancée, Kaitlan.

"What's the matter?" Marilyn asked behind him, her sudden presence nearly causing him to jump.

"I can't find what I'm looking for."

"Which is?"

When Jake didn't reply right away, Marilyn said, "You've heard the saying—everything you ever wanted to know, you'll find at the library. Well, who better to ask than the librarian?"

Why not? Jake asked himself. He didn't have to tell her everything. "Have you ever heard of Jacob Krinshaw?"

"Of course I have." He stiffened in surprise at her reply. "His father, Richard, started Krinshaw Shipping Company back before the turn of the century. We in the Historical Society, often speculate as to what happened to him."

"What do you mean 'what happened to him'?" Jake went still. He knew exactly what happened to him. If he allowed himself to think about it, he could still feel the rush of the cold water all around him, keeping him from breathing.

Marilyn shrugged. "Rumor has it, his father wanted him to run the company. But Jacob Krinshaw wanted to be an artist. They argued a great deal about it. And they were said to have had a huge fight on the Fourth of July. After that, Jacob disappeared. Many people think he took his fiancée and went West. But wherever he went, he never came back."

Jake was looking at her without really seeing her. He was seeing himself and Kate being pushed over the edge of that cliff to the rocks and raging sea below. Jake knew Jacob Krinshaw never came back. Neither did his fiancée. Because they were both dead.

"What do *you* think happened to him?" he asked, his throat so dry, his voice was tight.

"I think it was an accident, but I think Richard Krinshaw killed his own son after that fight," she replied without hesitation.

"Why?" Jake could barely speak.

"Because they say he became a bitter man after that, a totally changed man. And even though he hired investigators to find Jacob, he voiced his opinion several times that he didn't think Jacob would ever be found—as though he knew something no one else did. And there was the question of his will."

"His will?"

"He changed his will before the year ended, totally disinheriting Jacob, leaving everything to his second son. After that, apparently the police questioned him briefly about Jacob's disappearance. But there was never any evidence indicating foul play, much less that Richard had anything to do with it. You may find something about it in the issue of the *Times* the week of Thanksgiving," she explained.

Jake had to fight to swallow. He and Kate were the only people who knew what happened. The thought sent a shiver of cold fear up his back. "What happened to Richard?" he asked in a voice that sounded so far from his own.

"He never cared about the company after that, so I'm told. The younger son—his name was Nathaniel—took over and kept it from folding. He nearly lost it after the stock market crash in 1929. Krinshaw Shipping is now owned by his grandson, Michael. Richard died in 1921, after ten years of heavy drinking."

"Krinshaw Shipping is located about thirty miles down the coast, isn't it?" The memory came to Jake in a flash, just like all the others.

"Yes."

That put it between Willows Point and Port James, where Kate lived.

"It was relocated in 1933 or '34, I can't remember which," explained Marilyn.

Suddenly Jake started, hearing Kate's scream in his mind. "Kate!" He knew she was in trouble. He could feel her fear. He knew she wasn't sleeping any longer. But where was she? He couldn't see her. It was too dark. His own fear was well matched to hers. Damn, why hadn't he brought her with him where he could keep her safe?

"What's the matter?" asked Marilyn, her eyes wide and her voice suddenly raised with fear.

Jake jumped up. "I have to use your phone." He raced to the phone on the desk and dialed his own number, even though he was certain Kate wouldn't answer. He had the feeling she was no longer at the houseboat, but he still couldn't see where she was. He slammed down the phone. "We have to go," he said. "I have to get home right now!" He was heading toward the door, feeling he was already too late.

Back on Jake's houseboat, Kate woke up.

She sat up, stretched and rubbed her eyes, taking a moment to remember where she was and how she got there. She remembered her night with Jake and smiled.

Then she saw the note and the single red rose on the pillow beside her.

"How romantic," she said, reaching for them both at the same time.

She touched the soft petals of the bud to her nose, inhaling the sweet fragrance before her eyes moved to the words on the paper she held.

The paper was heavy and thick. The script was much more elegant than what Kate would have expected of Jake. The words were simple, but very direct.

I'll meet you at the carousel, my love.

"How sweet!" Kate nearly giggled, filled with the sudden excitement of a schoolgirl experiencing her first love. It was an exhilarating feeling, and Kate, holding the note and rose close, threw back the covers and jumped out of bed.

"My love," she muttered out loud, repeating the last two words of the note. She felt like his love. She felt as if she'd been his love forever. And the face that stared back at her from the mirror in his bathroom reflected that love in its rosiness and the shine in the eyes.

A short time later, Kate stepped out into a simply glorious day. The sun was shining, the rain gone. The warm breeze touched her with the strong feeling and sense of the sea. And it was easy to put fear aside.

Jake's car was gone, but that was fine. Kate wanted to walk and the carousel wasn't that far. She walked as fast as she could, without running. She wanted to reach Jake. She wanted to throw her arms around him and feel him against her. She wanted to look into his eyes and see his love there. She had to hold herself back to keep from skipping.

She reached the building that housed the carousel and slid the door open. "Jake?" she called. No reply reached her. The large room was dark and empty, except for the horses of the carousel, which looked to Kate to be standing guard. They seemed to be waiting and watching.

She stepped into the room, holding her rose in one hand. Her heart quickened its pace for no reason as she looked at the horses. Was that gray one looking at her? Her overwhelming feeling of happiness was quickly being washed away into fear, a fear she couldn't explain. Did that white horse with the broken mane move? It looked as if it did. Kate felt the hair on the back of her neck rise.

This is silly, she tried to tell herself. Jake isn't here. He went for paint or something, that's all. She'd just step out, close the door and leave. She'd wait for him at his houseboat. No problem.

A sudden gust of wind hit her. She jumped and nearly stumbled, thinking someone had actually touched her. Her heart raced then as she realized that gust came from *inside* the building. Fear swept through her like a giant tidal wave. She had to get out, she had to get away from those horses now. She felt that if she didn't, they were all going to come to life and trample her. She took a step back.

But before she could move farther, the heavy, rusted door slid closed on its own and she was engulfed in darkness. In one terrifying moment, Kate screamed, her voice echoing through the dark, empty building.

For several long seconds, Kate stood completely still, certain that at any moment she would hear the pounding hooves of the horses coming at her. She did hear a pounding, but it was her own heart. The door was right behind her. She silently thanked her lucky stars that she was able to keep her head together enough to remember that. She turned toward the door and tried to pull it open. It refused to move. The darkness was so thick, Kate couldn't breathe. Her heart was racing so fast, she could nearly feel pain in her chest. And she was trying desperately to draw in a much-needed breath. But all the oxygen seemed to have been wiped out with the light. She closed her eyes against the darkness, still pulling against that heavy door with all her strength.

She did, indeed, feel a touch then. It was the touch of a warm, live hand that came to rest on her shoulder.

CHAPTER TEN

Kaitlan jumped away from the hand and turned in a snap, her eyes open instantly.

She stopped short, staring at what she saw. The room was again filled with lights and noise and people, all of whom were going about their own business and not paying any attention to Kaitlan.

Except for the man who'd touched her shoulder.

It was John, from the dreams, and Kaitlan didn't like the way he was glaring down at her. She felt there was something about him she should know, but she couldn't remember what it was. She stared up at him.

His eyes were dark and intense, reminding her of some sort of bird. A hawk, perhaps. Or a vulture.

"Waiting for him again, I see, dear Kaitlan," he snapped.

"It's none of your business," she replied with an equal amount of venom in her voice. She tried to turn away, but to her horror, he took her arm and prevented her from doing so. "It's rather stuffy in here," she went on. "Let go of me. I wish to wait outside with Mr. and Mrs. Krinshaw."

"Don't you realize you'll be waiting for your dear Jacob forever?" he asked, his voice harsh and only loud enough for her to hear over the noise of the crowd. "He can't seem to slither out from beneath his father's heel."

"Let go of me!" she demanded.

He smiled for the first time, but it put no warmth in those dark eyes. And he let her go. "I'm sorry, Kaitlan. I shouldn't have done that."

Kaitlan watched him with cautious eyes for a moment then turned away to go back outside to find Mr. and Mrs. Krinshaw. John's words stopped her.

"He sent me to get you."

She turned back to him hesitantly. "He did?"

Still smiling, he nodded. "Yes. I was walking past the shipping office, and he motioned me in. He said he might be a little longer than he expected and he wanted you with him. He asked that I bring you."

"But he left me a note and this rose asking me to meet him here." She held up the rose for him to see.

"I don't know anything about a note. But he bought the rose from me earlier. And he just asked that I bring you to the office, and of course I agreed without any hesitation."

"You're not lying to me?" she asked.

"I'm insulted," he replied shortly, "that you would think me a liar."

"I'm sorry," she said quickly.

She thought for a moment, her eyes moving around the large room. "All right," she said finally. "You may take me to him."

"It will be my pleasure, sweet Kate."

He offered his arm, and Kaitlan took it hesitantly. "It's Kaitlan, John. Not Kate."

"Of course."

He led her out into the night, and they moved up the walk in the direction of Krinshaw Shipping offices. Kate had been there several times in the past week and she knew the way well. Because everything was so familiar to her, she lowered her guard. Not much, but enough that when John suddenly pulled her into a small alleyway between two tall buildings, she was caught unaware. He pressed her up against the cold wall of the building with his hardness before she even had time to think.

His hard, demanding mouth came crashing down on her soft, tender lips.

Kaitlan had never experienced such an overwhelming sense of violation. She didn't think. She did not have the time. Her instincts took over, and she reacted without thought. He had her pressed against the building with his whole body and there was little way in which she could move. Yet the small movement she had was enough and effective. She brought the heel of her shoe down on his instep with all the strength she could muster.

John cried out in pain and jerked away. Kaitlan took the opportunity to sweep away from him and dash out of the alley back onto the walkway. The street was well lit with many lamps, and the carousel house was not far away. Kaitlan silently thanked God that John hadn't led her any farther. She made her way quickly back to the crowd, the lights and the music.

Heat was radiating within her, and she felt the warm rush of blood in her cheeks. Whether it was from running or from the humiliation of John's actions, she had no idea. She only knew that she felt suddenly and totally alone. She could not see Jacob's parents. Or Jacob. Or any other familiar face for that matter. For one brief moment, she thought of what John had almost done to her, and a great sob of shame rose in her throat. She closed her eyes and forced it down with a swallow. She took a deep breath and tried to pat down the tawny wisps of hair that had escaped the pins near the top of her head. She must look a fright, she thought. She looked around, still seeing no one she recognized. But she did notice something else.

John was returning, making his way back to the carousel house, coming in her direction.

She had to do something. Her heart was pounding again and her mind was racing. She looked around frantically and saw no one who could help her, even though the room and the area outside were filled with people.

The carousel was stopping, she saw. Its present riders were climbing off.

Kaitlan moved toward it. The man who operated it smiled at her and tipped his felt cap. She climbed onto the platform and then onto a black horse with a red saddle. She'd ride the carousel for an hour if she had to wait that long for Jacob. Oh, please, Jacob, come soon, she pleaded silently. All the while she forced herself to smile and look happy. She knew she'd be safe as soon as Jacob arrived.

The carousel started. Kaitlan held the pole and rode the horse, trying to let the music fill her thoughts. She watched the faces that waited in the crowd. She watched the little girl on the horse beside her, who giggled merrily. She saw John watching her amid the crowd. His eyes were hard, but his expression told her he could wait, that he would wait. Kaitlan didn't look at him on the next two trips around.

On the third trip, Kaitlan's world brightened and she had true reason to smile. Jacob's friend, Anthony, stood near John. On his arm was that sweet lady friend of his, but Kaitlan couldn't remember her name just then. She thought it was Marilee or Marla or something like that. She waved, and Anthony waved back, shouting hello to her. She purposely didn't let her eyes fall on John.

On the next trip around, her heart actually fluttered, for Jacob stood next to them. She'd never been so glad to see him in her life. The love she felt for him poured out of her with every breath she took, and she couldn't wait for the carousel to stop so she could reach him and touch him. She waved again.

She knew he loved her, and the knowledge filled her, allowing her to forget about John and what he'd tried to do. She decided right then she would not allow John to ruin the rest of her stay with Jacob and his parents. She would not tell Jacob what John had done. She'd simply concentrate on the love they had for each other and the happiness he gave her. She saw Jacob and Anthony speak, and whatever Jacob said made the others laugh. His gaze then met hers across the room, and he blew her a kiss.

The carousel stopped, and Kaitlan slid down the side of the horse. She nearly ran through the crowd to reach him, and she melted against him.

"I love you, Jacob," she said, looking up at him, holding on to him as though she couldn't touch him enough.

Jacob laughed that warm, full laugh of his. "If that's what the carousel does to you, my sweet, I shall bring you here every day to ride it."

"That's enough out of you two lovebirds," said Anthony, a wide grin on his face. "Besides, I'm ready for an ice-cream cone, and your display of emotion is keeping me from it."

Jacob smiled down at her tenderly. "Shall we walk to the park?" he asked. "We probably have time for a dance or two before the fireworks start."

Kaitlan felt lost in the deepness of his brown eyes. She nodded, unable to speak.

"Let's not forget about the ice cream," piped Anthony from behind Jacob.

Not that Kaitlan was watching John, but she couldn't help but notice that he didn't follow them. She was glad. She never wanted to see him again. She thought briefly once more of telling Jacob, then decided against it. It would only make him angry. And she wanted nothing to spoil this night or the rest of their time together. She'd be taking the train home in a few days, and it might be weeks before they were able to see each other again.

They walked to the park, taking their time, laughing at their conversation. The men flirted in their own way, and the women flirted back. It was easy for Kaitlan to fall back into her dream world of love.

"I'm sorry I was so late," Jacob said sincerely.

"And there I was almost afraid you'd forgotten me," Kate replied, pretending to pout.

Jacob laughed again. "I could never forget you, my love. I could no sooner cut off my own hand than let you go, my sweet thing."

She smiled up at him, sensing his love for her throughout her whole body.

They reached the park. Kaitlan could feel the strength in Jacob's arms, and the smile that remained on her lips was genuine. She was happy, and the world was once again a perfect place.

They passed under the Willows Point Independence Day banner and drew close to the crowd and the noise and the music.

"Dance with me, Kaitlan," Jacob said. "I need to hold you close, and it's the only publicly acceptable way."

"Can't it wait?" asked Anthony.

Kaitlan giggled, holding Jacob's arm.

"No," replied Jacob.

"Well, we're going to get some ice cream." Anthony tried to sound angry, but there was amusement in his voice.

"We'll meet you at the ice-cream booth then," Jacob said absently. He strode off in the direction of the pavilion and the music, taking Kaitlan with him.

Anthony and Marilee—Kaitlan had remembered her name—went off in another direction through the crowd.

Jacob and Kaitlan joined the dancing crowd, and he took her in his arms.

Kaitlan danced, following his every step. She met his gaze, feeling the world couldn't be better. He smiled down at her, and her heart felt as though it were singing with the music.

Then suddenly it ended.

Jacob stopped dancing because someone tapped him on the shoulder. Kaitlan felt her eyes widen, seeing John standing there.

"May I cut in?"

"But of course," replied Jacob politely, before Kaitlan had the chance to even open her mouth. "Kaitlan," he said, turning back to her, his gaze filled with such tenderness, she could have cried. "I see my father right over there—" he looked out the pavilion past her shoulder "—and I need to talk to him. So I'll be right back."

He was gone almost before Kaitlan realized he was leaving. And John swept her into his arms in one smooth move.

Then it was too late; she was caught in his grasp.

She worked to catch up with his step and she closed her eyes, not wanting to go any further, not wanting to feel herself in his arms while they danced. Memories came to her then. Or were they premonitions? Kaitlan wasn't sure. But the visions came, showing her with great detail just what was to happen. She knew he would later drag her away, only to fight with Jacob and push them both into the sea. A shudder passed through her.

When Kate opened her eyes, she found herself standing just above the steps on the pavilion. But it was daytime now, and the crowds were gone. There were no people, no music. The park was deserted. She saw no gas lamps, but streetlights and electrical poles. The pavilion looked older, worn from years of use and exposure. Its paint was peeling. Somehow—and Kate didn't even want to think of how—she'd gotten from the carousel to the park.

"Kate?"

She turned to meet deep brown eyes. Jake's eyes. He stood one step below her on the ground, and she was nearly at eye level with him. She stared at him through her own tear-filled eyes. She closed them for a moment, and the action forced a tear to slide silently down her cheek.

She opened her eyes and swallowed hard. Jake pulled her to him then, and Kate melted to fit against him.

"Tell me," he said. "Something happened. Something I couldn't see because Jacob Krinshaw never saw it, and I'm only seeing things through his eyes."

"He tried to hurt me before that night," Kate said, her words sounding slightly muffled because he held her face pressed against his neck and jacket. She no longer thought of herself and Jacob's fiancée, Kaitlan, as two separate people. So there seemed to be no reason not to refer to Jacob's fiancée as herself. She felt that everything John had done and said had been done and said to *her.*

"John?"

She nodded against him.

"When?"

"I went to the carousel house with your parents because you were working late," she explained. "He said he'd seen you, and you asked him to bring me to you. He pulled me into an alley, and—"

Jake swore loudly. "I'm so sorry, Kate," he said as though he, Jake Casperson, had been responsible and that it had really happened to Kate McCoy.

She shivered in his arms.

"Come on," he said. He still held one arm around her as he led her away from the pavilion. They moved together through the park toward the street.

"Where are we going?" she asked in a small voice. These visions, or whatever they were, always left her feeling drained of all her energy. She leaned against him and let him help her walk.

"To Anthony's. It's closer than the boat. He'll have some hot coffee there to warm you up." And he will probably also have a thousand questions, Jake thought.

"Something hot sounds really good," she said. She felt as though her insides were shivering. She felt so cold, so empty and cold.

"Where's your car?" she asked, trying to match his steps. She clenched her teeth to keep them from chattering.

"At the carousel house." He was looking ahead. Kate looked ahead, too. She could see Anthony's.

"How did you know where to find me?" She had to ask.

He shrugged. "The same way I know everything else, I guess. I didn't even look inside the carousel house to see you weren't there. I already knew. Then my legs just started walking, and I knew exactly where to go."

They reached Anthony's. The door was locked, however, and the Closed sign hung on the front window.

Jake ignored both and knocked loudly with the bottom end of his closed fist.

After several long seconds, Kate heard the locks being turned, and Anthony opened the door.

"What's up?" he asked, looking at Jake. "You know I'm closed on Sundays until four o'clock." His eyes shifted to Kate, then widened. "What the hell did you do to her, Jake?" he asked, his voice filled with sudden alarm. "She looks like she's either half-frozen or she's seen a ghost. Come on in here." He stepped aside so they could come in and he locked the door behind them.

Jake nearly laughed, thinking Anthony had no idea what he'd just said. And he almost told Anthony that he was right on both counts. Instead, he merely asked, "Could we have some coffee, and maybe some of that bread you always keep on hand? We haven't had anything to eat since we were here yesterday."

Anthony stared at them both for another moment, not believing what he'd just heard. "Sure," he said finally. "The coffee will take a few minutes. But I can pop some bread in the microwave and warm it in a flash."

"Thanks," Jake muttered. He led Kate to a booth and slid in beside her when she sat down. He sat close and held her, refusing to let her go, trying to warm her with his own body heat.

Anthony watched them with concern spread all over his face. Then he swept into the kitchen and was gone.

"Kate," Jake said softly. "You have to tell me everything. Because I can't see it. I can only see what Krinshaw saw."

"I know," she said. She took a deep breath and told him everything she could remember, starting with how she went to the carousel with his parents, how John persuaded her to go with him and then pulled her into the alley and kissed her.

Jake laughed bitterly. "He nearly told me," he said. "When you were on that carousel, he said someone was going to steal you away from me. How could I have been so blind?" His voice raised in anger. "And you were afraid of him, but I just ignored it. I nearly pushed you into his arms when he asked to dance with you. If only I had kept you with me."

Kate shook her head. "We can't change any of it. I mean I could say a lot of ifs, too. If only I'd told you. If only I'd stayed near your parents. I could go on." She leaned against him, placing her head against the hard muscle of his upper arm. It was hard and soft at the same time, like a firm pillow cushioning her with its strength.

Then Jake shifted his position, taking his arm out from under her. He wrapped it around her and drew her close against his side, where she now rested her head. It reminded her of the way he held her close after making love with her.

Anthony returned, finding them that way. He carried a tray. "I had some French onion soup left over from yesterday," he said, placing the tray on the table. "And of course, I've got lots of bread." He set bowls, small plates and utensils on the table.

"So," he said as he sat down opposite them, "are you two going to tell me what's going on?"

"I kept her out in the rain too long, that's all," Jake said, lying easily.

Anthony chuckled. "Right," he said, his voice filled with sarcasm. He was quiet for a moment while he cut the bread for them.

Kate moved out of Jake's hold just enough to eat the soup sitting before her. Its strong aroma was enough to send her empty stomach into grumbles of hunger. She took a spoonful without meeting Anthony's eyes across the table, and burned her mouth. She swallowed it as quickly as possible and succeeded in burning her throat as well.

Beside her, Jake absently stirred his soup around the melted cheese that covered most of the bowl before taking a spoonful. Smart man, she thought. She blew on the next spoonful before sticking it in her mouth.

"The coffee's probably ready." Anthony got up and went back to the kitchen.

"How much do you plan to tell him?" Kate asked. She was poking her spoon through the bread and melted cheese covering her soup.

Jake turned to her, and when he spoke, his breath was warm on her temple. "I don't know that I should tell him anything. I mean, we've been friends forever, but I wouldn't want him to think that I've lost my mind."

They were quiet, and Anthony returned carrying the same tray, which now held three mugs of steaming coffee. He set one before each of them as he sat down again. "You know, Jake," he said, "she's bound to be sick if you keep dragging her out in the rain." He held Jake's gaze. "Not to mention, I haven't been outside much today, but I don't think it's rained a drop since early this morning. And I mean real early—like right after midnight." He paused and took a sip of black coffee.

"We were hoping your soup would warm us up enough so we won't get sick," replied Jake.

Anthony set his mug down on the table with a heavy thud. "Dammit, Jake!" he snapped. "Are you going to tell me what the hell's going on, or am I going to have to tie you up in the kitchen and torture it out of you?"

"Just what makes you think something's going on?" Jake asked evenly.

Kate hardly looked up from her soup. She wondered how Jake could look at Anthony and lie so well. Even though he wasn't actually lying with his last question, Kate knew that if she met Anthony's gaze, her eyes would tell him everything. So she just stared at her bowl of soup. And when she took a sip of coffee, she stared at her mug as well.

"I'll tell you what," Anthony snapped, even though he managed to keep his voice low. "You come in here yesterday and act really strange. You tell me you're engaged, and Kate appears just as surprised as I am. Then you show up today looking like hell. To top it off, I feel like I haven't slept a minute all night, so I'm not in the best of moods." His eyes moved from Jake to Kate. Kate was looking up at him now, unable to tear her gaze away. Jake had stopped stirring his soup and was looking hard at Anthony, too.

"You had trouble sleeping?" Kate asked, feeling as if the soup were suddenly sticking in her throat.

Anthony raked a hand through his hair, leaving it all standing up. "I had one of the strangest dreams I've ever had. It felt so real, as if I really lived it. After I woke up, I walked around my apartment, looking at all my modern appliances, the microwave, the television, even my electric toothbrush. I had the strangest feeling that if I didn't see for myself that I still had them, I wasn't living in this modern age of technology anymore."

Kate turned and looked up at Jake. Her heart was pounding in her chest. He met her eyes briefly. Whatever was happening to them was happening to Anthony, too. She had the mad urge to lean up and kiss Jake, to feel his lips touching hers. She had no idea why. It just seemed that the need to be close always came along with the fear.

Jake, reading her mind as usual, touched her leg under the table. His one-word message came to her silently. *Later.*

Anthony broke their thoughts. "So are you going to tell me what's going on?"

"Tell us about the dream first," Jake said. For the first time, Kate met Anthony's eyes evenly across the table. She felt stronger now. She felt her fear lessen. There were three of them now to face this, and the idea that they weren't alone made it easier to face.

"Why are you interested in some stupid dream?"

"We just are," Jake replied. "Humor us."

"Why?" Anthony asked again. "Are you doing a study or something?"

"No," Jake said, his voice revealing for the first time his impatience. "Just tell us."

Anthony shrugged. "There's not much excitement to it, really. Marilyn and I walked into that building where the carousel is, the one you're painting. Everyone was dressed funny, in long dresses. Marilyn even had this hat on with feathers on it." He chuckled at the memory. Kate smiled, remembering the hat as well.

"Kate was riding the carousel, waving to us," he went on, looking at Kate, who had stopped eating for a moment. "Then you came in and said something about work, and I said, 'a man's work is never done.' I said that yesterday, remember?"

"Yes," Jake replied. "Why do you think you had the dream, Anthony?"

He shrugged again. "I don't know. I mean, why do any of us dream what we dream?"

"Are you dating Marilyn?" Jake asked, feeling he already knew the answer.

"She invited me over for dinner today, Jake. And don't say a word about it. She's worried about people finding out," Anthony replied, giving Jake a hard look.

"Why?" asked Kate.

"She's got some hang-up about her being the librarian and me owning a business in town. She's worried some people might get the wrong impression, and she wants to keep it quiet for a while." He fingered his coffee mug absently and paused for a moment. "So tell me why you're so interested in some silly dream I've had."

"We've had the same dream," Jake said simply.

Anthony's gaze met Jake's before locking on to Kate's. The room was dead quiet. "That's impossible," he whispered.

"It's true," Kate informed him.

"Two people cannot have the same dream."

Kate nearly laughed. She did smile. "I said the same thing."

Anthony's eyes widened in surprise, his brows rose. "I don't believe this. Both of you had the same dream?"

"Yes." This time they both replied together.

"How did you do this?" Anthony looked back at Jake. "Did you plant some little bug in my brain or something?"

"No," said Jake.

"Then how?" Anthony demanded, his voice full of anger.

Kate nearly smiled again, remembering how she'd welcomed that feeling of anger, too. Anger was so much easier to accept. "We didn't do anything," she said softly, remembering, too, that the fear was easier to handle when she realized she wasn't alone.

Anthony laughed a harsh, bitter laugh. "Then you're trying to tell me that we've all gone crazy together, is that it? Should we call the ambulance now or after you've finished your soup?"

Kate turned and met Jake's gaze for a moment. They understood Anthony's fear, for it was still just as real to them. Under the table, Jake's hand rested on Kate's leg. "Tell us what else you remember about the dream."

Anthony sighed. "We went to a Fourth of July celebration in the village park."

"You wanted ice cream," Kate pointed out.

Anthony looked hard at her. His forgotten coffee sat before him cooling. "This is... impossible," he said finally. The words came out slowly.

"That's what we keep telling each other, too," said Jake.

Kate laughed at that comment. It felt good to laugh. It felt good to be able to laugh. The laughter and the warm food gave Kate a much lighter feeling.

"You really had the same dream?" Anthony asked slowly.

"The very same," said Kate. She felt the strong desire to reach out and take Anthony's hand. She remembered the fear she'd felt when she first began having the dreams, and she remembered her own need to reach out and grasp someone, anyone who could give her some stability.

Jake's mental message came to her. *Go ahead, honey, take his hand. He needs us.*

Kate took Anthony's hand. He grasped hers tightly, like a drowning man clinging to a life ring. She offered him an understanding smile.

"Why?" Anthony's question came out in a harsh breath.

"We think the dreams are trying to lead us to someone," Jake explained.

"Who?" It was another harsh question, coming through a tight throat.

"John Tallon," Kate said simply, even though she felt a tremor of terror pass through her just at the sound of his name.

Anthony took a deep breath, still holding Kate's hand. "Why?" he asked again, sounding somewhat clearer this time, but only a little.

"Because he's a killer," Jake said evenly. "That's why."

CHAPTER ELEVEN

"A killer?" echoed Anthony, looking at them with bewildered shock.

Jake didn't explain anything more. He asked a question of his own. "Who did you walk to the village park with?"

Anthony swallowed hard. "You and Kate and Marilyn." He stopped and thought for a moment. "But I called you Jacob, not Jake, and Kate was Kaitlan. And Marilyn was Marilee."

Jake nodded. "It wasn't really me," he said. He was trying to convince himself of the fact as well, for he could still feel the cold saltwater rush over him if he let the thought enter his mind. "It was Jacob Krinshaw."

Anthony looked at them, unblinking. "Krinshaw? That name sounds familiar."

Jake explained quickly about the Krinshaw Shipping Company.

Kate listened, still eating the soup and bread. When she reached for a second piece of bread, Anthony absently pushed the plate closer to her.

"So what makes you think this guy, John Tallon, is a killer?" Anthony asked.

Kate had no idea whether Anthony believed anything Jake was telling him. But he was greatly intrigued with the tale.

"He pushed both Jacob Krinshaw and his fiancée, Kaitlan, over the cliff up near the lighthouse," said Jake.

"Into the sea?" Anthony's eyes widened.

Jake nodded.

"Both of you—them?"

It was clear that the dream had impressed Anthony enough that he wasn't sure whether or not Jake and Jacob Krinshaw were the same person, even if he didn't quite believe the rest of the story. His gaze shifted to Kate.

"Yes," Jake replied, sounding somewhat out of breath.

Kate knew what he was feeling. He was feeling the cold, black sea washing over him, dragging him down, taking him away into nothingness. She felt his fear, strong and bitter. The fear itself was nearly as frightening as the act of falling into the sea. She hadn't realized until then just how important it had been for her to wake up. If she hadn't awakened herself by rolling off the couch, both she and Jake would probably be dead. That thought brought a whole new wave of fear over her, filling her with coldness.

"Damn!" Anthony muttered. He was looking at them both with wide, astonished eyes. "How do you know this? Did you *really* dream it, too?"

"Yes," said Jake.

"Both of you?"

It was Kate's turn to reply between bites. "Yes." Her soup was nearly gone, and she was tempted to ask for more.

"You were there with John at the carousel before I arrived," said Jake. "Did he say anything to you?"

Anthony looked at Kate. "He pointed out Kate. Kaitlan," he corrected. "On the carousel."

Jake looked over at Kate, too. "He must be obsessed with you."

Kate could still feel John's lips pressing against hers, violating her in a way she'd never felt before. "That's putting it mildly," she replied. To Kate, it was no longer just a dream. In fact, the realness of the visions was intensifying as time went on.

Anthony looked at his watch. Kate got another mental message from Jake. *Anthony has a date, Kate. We have to go.*

Kate smiled across the table at him. "Thanks for the soup, Anthony. It was really good."

"How much do I owe you?" asked Jake.

"Forget it," Anthony replied. He was still sitting there, a dazed expression on his face. Kate remembered feeling that way when she'd fixed breakfast the day before.

"I promised Kate I'd take her home this afternoon."

"That's fine, Jake," Anthony muttered. "Will you come back tonight so we can talk about this more?"

"I don't know," Jake replied slowly. He was filled with the strange sensation that he wouldn't be coming back to Willows Point. At least not tonight. He wondered if it was simply because he'd be staying with Kate, or if something more drastic, more final was about to happen to him.

Kate broke his thoughts. "We could stay a while now and talk more about it if you want." Her voice was soft, calm. She obviously didn't get any feeling that something was going to happen. Jake didn't know if he should feel grateful or not.

"No, that's all right," said Anthony. He scratched his temple absently. "I don't think I'm ready to talk any more about this right now, anyway. I don't even want to think about it. I just want to spend some quiet time with Marilyn before I have to open."

Kate smiled at him. She nearly wished him luck, remembering how hard she'd tried to ignore the dreams and Jake and the fear. They helped Anthony take the dirty dishes into the kitchen before they said goodbye and left. They walked back toward the boardwalk, needing to go to the carousel for Jake's car.

"Do you think he'll be all right?" Kate asked. She hated leaving Anthony looking so confused and uneasy. She remembered the feeling so well, and she also remembered how it was Jake's presence that had brought a sense of stability.

Jake took her hand. "I think so. I think he needs to be with Marilyn. Just like you and I needed to be together."

"I hope you're right," she said slowly. "Did our eyes look that haunted?"

"Probably."

The sun was still out, still fighting the clouds that tried to overtake it. And Kate raised her face toward it, allowing what little warmth it gave to touch her. "Have you had a hard time feeling warm since the dreams started?"

Jake was silent, thinking about the question.

Kate explained further. "Like you want to stay really close to me, feeling my body heat. Or you want to eat hot foods and drink hot coffee or tea."

Jake looked over at her without slowing his steps. "Yes, now that you mention it," he replied finally. He remembered that strange chill that had passed over him when he'd studied the drawing of the carousel horse earlier. But he said nothing of it.

"I think it goes along with the dreams, but I don't understand why," she put in.

Jake swallowed hard and still said nothing. *He* understood why, though. He understood it very well. The sea was cold. Just thinking about it brought goose bumps to his arms, and he fought away a shiver. He had the feeling death would be as cold, too. He had to fight away that thought. Since Kate hadn't actually been in the water as he felt he had, she couldn't possibly understand it. So Jake said nothing.

"Thanks for the rose," she said suddenly, her voice even lighter.

"You're welcome," he replied. "It looks nice on your table," he commented, thinking she meant the rose he'd left after the first dream.

"Not that one, silly." She nearly giggled. "The one you left on your pillow this morning. Along with that note." She felt heat touch her cheeks just thinking about that note. *My love.* Those words sang through her mind over and over.

Jake's next words, however, brought that singing to a screeching halt. "What rose? I left you a note, but I didn't leave a rose."

Kate stopped walking just as suddenly. "Of course you did. A red one. It was on the pillow next to me." Was he suddenly shy, playing hard to get? The thought nearly made her laugh.

His brows rose. "Where is it now, Kate?"

"I—" She stopped and thought for a long moment. Where was it? "I don't really know. I had it when I went to the carousel, but I don't remember where I dropped it."

Jake was still holding her hand. "Come on, maybe it's at the carousel." He tugged to get her moving.

"By the way," said Kate, "why weren't you there before?"

"Why wasn't I where before?" he asked in reply without looking at her.

She looked up at him. And he turned at the same time to look down at her. The heat of their gazes met and held, and their walking slowed slightly. "At the carousel."

Kate wasn't aware that her voice changed, that it grew deeper. Jake heard it and remembered the way it had done that while they'd made love. He realized her voice had deepened every time he kissed her. He couldn't help but smile down at her, and for a moment her words didn't quite register.

"At the carousel?" he echoed when those words finally reached him. "Why would you think I'd be there?"

"Because your note said you would," she replied simply. Oh, how she liked looking up at him. His profile radiated strength. The gold in his hair nearly sparkled. His eyes touched her with a sense of his gentle strength, and Kate wondered for a moment at the thought of what his children might look like. She knew they'd be beautiful. Sometimes when she looked at him, she felt like a totally different person. She had to be a different person. She couldn't possibly be the same person who'd experienced such a painful divorce and vowed to never let another man get close to her. Because she wanted to be close to Jake. She wanted to be close to him in every possible way. And she wasn't even afraid to be close to him. Not really. Not anymore. The sheer excitement of it overrode the fear.

But right now, fear did touch her with his words. "No, it didn't. The note I left you told you I was going to the library, which is where I went."

Kate actually felt the color drain from her face. Perhaps she was losing her mind. That thought nearly made her sick to her stomach. She shook her head slowly against his shoulder. "No," she insisted. "It said to meet me at the carousel."

"Kate," he said, his voice just as stubborn, "I know what I wrote." He rattled off his words about going to the library and being back in time to make her lunch.

"No," she still insisted. Her voice rose with fear, and that one simple word came out a little shaky. She heard it herself and didn't like the sound.

Suddenly everything around her became crystal clear.

"This was all a setup, wasn't it?" she whispered. She pulled out of his arms at the same time. "Some sort of game set up to drive me crazy."

"No, it wasn't." Jake tried to reach for her, but she slipped out of his grasp.

"Why are you doing this?" she went on. "All I have is my house, my car, my job and a life-insurance policy that couldn't possibly be worth the time and effort."

"I never set you up." Jake fought desperately to keep his voice even.

She stopped walking, and so did he. She was glaring at him, her eyes spitting angry fire. And Jake was doing his best to stay in control. The last thing he wanted to do was quarrel right out in the middle of town, yelling about a topic that would make everyone who heard them think they were both crazy.

"Right," she replied sarcastically.

"Do you think I could have set those dreams in your subconscious, Kate? Do you really think that?"

She didn't reply.

"And what about Anthony?" His voice was tight with his effort to keep from yelling. "Do you think I could have set him up, too?"

"You could be in this together," she said, her tone filled with venom. "He could be lying."

"Oh, yes, he sure looked like he was lying." It was Jake's turn to be sarcastic. "If that's the case, he should close up shop and fly to Hollywood tomorrow."

"All I know is the more I'm around you, the clearer these visions become," she went on, her breathing sounding labored with anger, frustration and fear. "And I also know that it's always been you, Jake, who's broadened them. You first mentioned walking under that banner, about it being 1911 when I didn't remember. You brought up the fact that I let you in the back door for that first dream. You always seemed to remember what I couldn't."

"Kate," he put in, "I was only telling you what I remembered."

Kate shook her head, refusing to believe him. "Who put you up to this?" she asked. "Is it really one of those government experiments like I first thought? Were you sent to observe me?"

"No!" he nearly yelled, then looked around to see if anyone was close enough to hear.

"Is someone paying you?" Kate wanted to cry at that thought. "Is it some sort of research study, and I'm the guinea pig?"

"No."

She ignored him. "Just how much are you getting paid? And are you getting paid to sleep with me, too, or is that just an added bonus, like a vacation?" She blinked, trying to keep tears from spilling down her cheeks.

He'd heard enough. "Damn!" He tried to grab her, to pull her into his car where they could talk in private. But she managed to avoid his grasp. And after a glaring look, she turned and walked away from him.

He caught up with her.

"Kate!" He sighed heavily and tried to take her hand. She pulled it away.

"Don't touch me." She wouldn't look at him.

He walked to match her speed. "Kate, I promise you this is no setup," he said evenly, forcefully.

She said nothing. He reached out and grabbed her arm, and this time she let him.

Kate finally looked at him, seeking any sign that he might be lying to her. She studied him hard and saw no signs.

"I promise you," he said again, praying she'd believe him. "I am just as lost in this as you are. And so is Anthony."

She didn't want to believe him. She didn't want to believe that the three of them could be caught up in such a nightmare. It was easier to believe that it might be a government-controlled experiment, even as horrifying as that sounded. Yet she had no choice but to believe him. She had no choice but to stay with him and trust him. She was even more terrified at the thought of what could happen if she didn't. "If I find out you're lying to me," she said slowly, "I mean it, Jake, you'll never be more sorry in your life."

Seeing the look in her eyes, Jake didn't doubt that for a minute. Then something else caught his attention. The smell of pastry.

Kate frowned at the sudden change in his expression. Jake was tense, she could almost see the tension pulsing through his body. Without thinking, she reached out again and took his hand. "What's the matter, Jake?" she asked. She didn't understand why he suddenly turned around. Still holding her hand, he pulled her with him. They were standing in front of a bakery, and Jake was staring in the window with frightening intensity.

"Hungry, Jake?" she teased.

He didn't answer right away. When he did, his words came slowly. "Krinshaw Shipping was located here. In this building. Don't you remember, Kate?"

Kate looked in the window. The sweet aroma of pastry touched her. Then through the sweet smell came a memory. The memory of how the room had looked before, with large rolltop desks instead of shelves of doughnuts and tarts. The floor was wood, as well as the paneling. There were even electric lights hanging from the ceiling.

"Yes, I remember," she whispered. The idea of Jake setting her up was forgotten just as quickly as the vision had set in.

Jake was staring in through the window, and Kate knew he wasn't seeing the pastry. He was seeing the Krinshaw Shipping office. To Kate, it was nothing more than a memory. But it seemed much more to Jake. She supposed it was because it had been so much more to Jacob Krinshaw.

"We need to go there," he muttered.

"Krinshaw Shipping?"

"I think so." He finally turned from the window and looked at her. Were there tears in his eyes? "And to the house where the Krinshaws lived, too."

"Why there?" Kate's heart began to race at the thought of seeing that house, and she wasn't exactly sure why. It wasn't quite fear that was filling her, it was more like anticipation. Like a slide show, memories passed through her mind. There was a flash of a huge tiled foyer with a large chandelier hanging above and a wide, curved staircase. Then a large bedroom with a yellow canopied bed, a dining room with a long table. Kate knew there were enough chairs to seat fifty people.

Jake's reply caused her heart to race faster. "Because we have to go home, that's why. Krinshaw and his fiancée never went home again. We have to go home for them."

He still held her hand, and he gave it a gentle squeeze. "Come on, let's go."

They were walking again. "Are we just going to go up and knock on the front door?" Kate asked. She almost had to run to keep up with him.

"Yes." Their footsteps sounded loud on the boards of the walk.

Kate glanced over at him, and her gaze swept past something else. Something that caused her to stop suddenly again. This time, Jake moved right past her.

"What is it, Kate?"

Kate was looking at the large space between two buildings. One building held an accounting office. The other was empty with a large For Lease sign in the front window. But it was the alley between them that held Kate's attention.

"This is where John took me," she said slowly. The memory was so real, she felt out of breath, and her throat was tight with fear. She could still feel the hardness of his body pressed up against her. She could still feel his lips hurting hers. A swift wave of nausea rose up in her when she thought of his tongue in her mouth. She looked at the wall of the building that housed the accounting office, knowing the exact place on the bricks where her back had touched it. And she shivered.

Then her gaze moved down to the ground, and she gasped at what she saw there. She closed her eyes, breathing deep to keep from throwing up the soup she'd just eaten.

Jake followed her gaze to see the single red rose lying on the ground. He stared at it for a long moment, noticing that its petals looked oddly torn as though it had really been held during the struggle between Kaitlan and John.

Kate was holding his hand as tightly as she could, and her breathing sounded labored. Jake turned and pulled her into his arms, to calm her with his embrace. "It's all right, Kate," he said softly, trying to believe the words himself.

"I was here, Jake. I was really here." That thought was just as frightening as the assault on Kaitlan in the vision.

Jake was filling with fear, too. Fear for Kate. Fear for both of them at knowing that whatever this calling was, it was growing so strong, controlling them to the point that they were doing things they didn't even know they were doing. And the fear was coming from somewhere else, too. It was coming from a place deep inside him. A place where a tiny voice was telling him that they needed to go. Because they were running out of time...

"Come on, Kate, we have to go," he murmured into her ear. He kissed it as well.

They left the rose and moved on. Jake kept his arm around Kate, holding her as close to him as he could and still keep walking. They reached his car, and he helped her climb in.

They stopped at Jake's houseboat so Kate could show him the note she'd found on the pillow next to her. She distinctly remembered leaving it on the table. But it wasn't there. They quickly searched the rooms but found no trace.

"Are you sure you didn't take it with you like you did the rose?" Jake asked after he'd looked through the trash.

"I'm sure," she replied defensively. At least he didn't totally disbelieve her about the rose, she thought.

She leaned down to look under his bed and felt him touch her arm. He gently drew her back to her feet and took her in his arms. "Let's forget about it for now, Kate," he said softly against her ear. "Maybe I'll find it later."

Kate was pressed against him, enfolded in his arms, and she wouldn't have minded staying there forever. Everything about him touched her at once. His warmth. The husky, masculine smell she knew belonged to only him. The little electrical current that radiated from his fingertips right into her spine. Her senses came to life instantly.

"I'm just sorry I wasn't here to give you a proper good-morning when you woke up." He leaned down and touched his lips to hers, setting off an instant spark that seemed to pass through her entire body, leaving even the tips of her toes tingling.

It wasn't totally the truth, Jake thought, but he didn't tell her that. The truth was, he was sorry he hadn't been there to keep her from going to the carousel. He shouldn't have left her alone. He didn't think anything could top the fear he had of falling into the icy, black sea, but now his fear for Kate did. And it was an unexplainable fear. Something he didn't understand. He only understood it was there, and it gave him the sense that Kate was in more danger than he. And because of that fear, he was not going to let her out of his sight again. If he could, he would not let her out of the reach of his arms.

In his arms, Kate could not have felt safer. But she felt how tense he was. And she knew he was holding something back from her. She didn't push for it now. Something, some inner voice was telling her there simply was not time. "We should go." She hated herself for having to say it.

He kissed her once more, and he held her hand as they made their way to the car.

They said very little. Most of their talk centered around what Jake had learned at the library. But they never quit touching each other. They held hands. Kate held on to Jake's arm. Jake rested his hand on her knee. She rested hers on Jake's leg. Neither one really paid much attention to the fact; they just kept doing it.

They went to the Krinshaw family house first because it was closer. And it wasn't actually just a house. It was a mansion.

When the house came into view after nearly a mile of winding driveway, Kate gasped out loud. Jake just stared at it with wide eyes.

Jake followed the circle drive and stopped in front of the wide front door. They let go of each other just long enough to climb out of the car. Their eyes never left the massive stone structure before them, even as Jake came around the car to take her hand again.

"I've dreamed of this place," Kate said softly. "Ever since I was a kid." The hairs on the back of her neck were standing up.

"So have I," Jake whispered back.

Kate stared at the huge front door, expecting it to be opened by a tall, older man named Wilson, who would inform them that supper was waiting for them. She licked her suddenly dry lips, but her tongue and the rest of her mouth were just as dry. If she hadn't known better, she'd have thought her heart was running races through her chest. Despite the chilly, damp air, her hand felt wet in Jake's, but she refused to let him go.

Hesitantly, they moved to the front door. They stood before it, studying its detail.

"How do you feel?" Kate asked, her voice no more than a whisper.

"Like I'm coming home," Jake replied, his voice just as soft. Kate knew of no words to reply, so she merely offered him a quick, shaking smile.

The knocker on the door was the head of a lion. Jake raised the knocker and knocked three times. The sound echoed loudly inside.

They waited, still holding hands.

The door swung open, slowly, silently. The man who opened it stood tall and distinguished, wearing a black coat, but he was not the Wilson Kate had expected. "Can I help you?" he asked absently. Then his eyes shifted to Kate, and he stared at her, blinking as though he couldn't believe whom he was seeing.

Kate fought the mad urge to look down at herself to see what was causing him to look so surprised. She finally stopped smiling, closing her mouth in case she had food stuck between her teeth.

"We'd like to see Mr. Krinshaw," Jake said.

The man Kate assumed was a butler was still staring at her. "Of...course," he sputtered. Kate nearly laughed. It was funny to hear someone sputter like that when he looked so distinguished and in control.

He stepped aside and opened the door wider so they could enter the large foyer. The tile below their feet was black-and-white ceramic squares. A triple-tier crystal chandelier hung above their heads. Several feet in front of them a wide staircase curved, snaking its way to the second floor. Kate recognized it from past dreams. She knew the steps were marble. The wide, polished banister and its newel were cherry. Her gaze followed the staircase up.

She knew what was upstairs. Six bedrooms, each with its own bath, three on either side of the landing. At the far end of each hallway past the bedrooms was a sitting room. One was richly paneled in oak. The other was brighter, with soft comfortable furniture and flowered wallpaper. It had been Jacob Krinshaw's mother's favorite room, and Kaitlan had taken tea with Mrs. Krinshaw there many times during her visits. She knew that the stairs continued up, even though she couldn't see them from the foyer. On the third level, there were more bedrooms and a large nursery and playroom for children.

Kate looked around, memories flooding her mind. Jake was looking around, too.

The butler broke through her memories. "Do you have an appointment with Mr. Krinshaw?"

"No," Jake replied.

"Who shall I tell him is calling?" The butler was still staring at Kate.

"I'm Jake Casperson."

The butler's head turned to Jake so quickly, Kate thought he had to have twisted his neck in the process.

"And this is Kate McCoy."

The butler's head snapped back toward Kate just as quickly. His surprise was clearly written all over his face. "I s-see," he stammered. "Please wait right here." He looked at Kate for nearly another minute before turning and leaving through a pair of pocket doors.

"What do you suppose is wrong with him?" Kate whispered.

"Heck if I know," Jake muttered. His eyes were moving around again. "Can you get over this place?" His voice was filled with a mixture of anxiety, surprise and astonishment. He let go of her hand to step closer to that wide, beautiful staircase. "It's just like I remember."

Kate crossed her arms over her chest, feeling cold without his touch, and let out a huffed sigh. "I feel like I know what every single room looks like," she whispered.

"So do I." His words sounded like nothing more than an anxious breath. "But we don't. Not really. We know what they looked like in 1911. They could have had a major overhaul between then and now."

"The foyer didn't," Kate said. "The tile's the same. The stairs are the same."

"I know."

"It's frightening." Her voice shook. "It makes the dreams all so much more real. It makes Jacob and

Kaitlan real. So then their deaths are real, too. And then John's really a killer."

"I know," he said again, finally looking at her.

"Good afternoon, I'm Michael Krinshaw," a deep voice said from behind them.

Both Kate and Jake turned to the man standing there. He'd come through those pocket doors without a sound. Jake moved to stand next to Kate.

Michael Krinshaw was staring at Kate with dark, piercing eyes. "You're Kate McCoy?" he questioned.

"Yes."

He turned to Jake. "And Jake Casperson, is it?"

"Yes," Jake replied.

Michael watched them both for a long moment. "How can I help you?" he asked finally. His words were precise and touched with a definite New England accent. He was tall, with light golden brown hair and brown eyes.

"We'd like to talk to you, Mr. Krinshaw, regarding one of your ancestors. Jacob Krinshaw," said Kate nervously.

"Of course," he replied simply. The fact that he showed no surprise at Kate's words was a surprise in itself. Was this man having dreams, too?

He stepped closer. There was confidence and purpose to his movement. "But before you do, I think it's fair to let you know—" he looked directly at Kate "—you won't get what you want."

Kate blinked, trying to make sense of his words. She found his tone, laced with hostility, just as hard to understand. She stared back at him.

"And what is it you think we want?" Jake asked. He wasn't even sure himself just what they'd find there.

"Inheritance, of course." Michael said it so matter-of-factly that Kate's eyes widened in surprise.

"What inheritance?" she blurted before she was able to stop herself.

Michael Krinshaw chuckled. It was a deep, throaty laugh, but there was little warmth to it. "Your surprise looks so genuine."

"It is," Kate admitted. She had never felt more confused in her life. She recognized the man before her. He was definitely a descendant of Jacob Krinshaw. The eyes were nearly the same. Yet, not quite. Michael's eyes were piercing, cold enough to send a shiver up Kate's spine. Then she glanced at Jake. Jake's eyes were the same. Jake's eyes held the sparkle that Jacob Krinshaw's had. She supposed Jake and Michael, looking at each other, wouldn't be able to see any resemblance.

"Mr. Krinshaw," Jake put in, "we're not here to talk about any inheritance."

His eyes turned even colder and, for the first time, his expression revealed his surprise. "You're not?"

"No," Kate and Jake said at the same time.

"But it's obvious Miss McCoy is a distant relative of my great-uncle Jacob Krinshaw's fiancée," Michael said. "She even bears her name. But Jacob Krinshaw lost all chance of his inheritance when he left and Richard cut him out of the will. And so did any of his future relatives."

Jake looked at Kate, and she imagined her expression must match his in confusion. "Why do you think I'm a distant relative of hers?" she asked.

"Because you look just like her, that's why," Michael replied. "Now if you'll excuse me," he added, turning back to the pocket doors, which stood open behind him.

"I do?" Kate asked.

"She does?" Jake asked.

They both spoke at the same time, and their questions were enough to turn Michael back to face them. The puzzled look on his face was growing. He obviously didn't think they could fake their surprise as well as they were doing. "What is this? What's going on here?"

"Please, Mr. Krinshaw," Kate took a step forward. "We didn't come for any inheritance. Only information."

He was weary of her. "What information?"

"Information on Jacob and Kaitlan. Anything that you could tell us," she replied, stepping even closer to him.

Michael looked at her, then Jake. "Are you investigative reporters?"

Kate smiled, wishing it was that easy. "No, Jake's an artist, and I'm a schoolteacher."

The color drained from Michael's face, and Kate had the terrible feeling he might just faint and fall on the floor in front of her. "Mr. Krinshaw?"

"Come with me," he ordered, his voice raspy. He turned and went through that doorway with the hidden pocket doors into what Kate remembered Jacob called the drawing room.

Kate looked at Jake, then they both followed Michael.

The room wasn't much different from what Kate remembered. The wallpaper was a different print, yet still floral. The massive fireplace and the bookcases on either side appeared unchanged. Even a few of the pieces of furniture looked the same. Kate didn't really spend much time studying it. What caught her attention was the portrait over the fireplace. It held her captivated, her feet planted just inside the room.

Michael and Jake were staring at it, too.

"It was Jacob's last finished work," Michael explained, his voice sounding too loud in the room.

"Kaitlan," said Jake.

"Yes," said Michael. "He painted it shortly after he asked her to marry him in the spring of 1911, just before they disappeared."

Kate couldn't take her eyes from it. Kaitlan was beautiful, sitting in the garden Kate recognized as being behind this very house. She was wearing that blue-and-white-striped dress and holding a red rosebud on her lap.

Kate couldn't breathe. She thought she must be looking as if she might faint now. She tried to swallow, but there was nothing in her mouth to swallow. She felt her fists tightly clench, her palms sweating and clammy. She no longer thought her heart was racing, for it seemed to have stopped altogether the moment her eyes met that portrait.

Because Kaitlan's face and Kate's face were one and the same. Kate could have been looking into a mirror.

CHAPTER TWELVE

"She was a schoolteacher, too," Michael said slowly. He stood closer to the mantel than the others, closer to that painted image of Kaitlan, and he had to turn around to see Kate's reaction.

Kate had no reaction to the words. She was still staring at the painting in shock, unable to move, hardly able to breathe. She couldn't seem to tear her gaze away.

Kaitlan's eyes were looking at her, and for a moment Kate had the same feeling she'd had in the carousel house. She felt that Kaitlan was going to stand up and walk right out of the painting, just as she'd felt the horses of the carousel were going to come to life and trample her. She closed her eyes tightly. But her action brought about a surprising flash of a vision. It was very fast, and extremely detailed....

No fire burned in the fireplace, but the room was charged with the heat of an argument. Bright sunlight poured through the tall windows. Voices carried to Kaitlan.

"When Kaitlan and I are married in October, we'll be leaving, Father, and I will not be here to work for the company any longer."

The second voice was filled with even more anger, more energy. "If you do that, I will cut you out of my will so fast, your head will spin!"

Kate opened her eyes in a snap. Kaitlan was still sitting on the bench in the portrait. Jake reached out in a knowing gesture and took Kate's hand.

"You can understand the shock my butler felt when he saw you." Michael was still looking at her, studying her intently, his gaze still piercing, but now only filled with great interest. His words and the way he was looking at her brought her back to the present, forcing her to forget about the vision for the moment. "And you can understand why I would think you were after an inheritance."

"Yes," Kate said, but her throat was so dry, the simple word came out in a painful whisper. She swallowed hard, but it helped very little. When she felt she had enough voice, she asked, "Why was Jacob's father so bent on his running the company when he had a second son who turned out to be just as capable of doing the job?"

Michael shrugged absently. "I don't know. Maybe it was one of those first-son bonding things. I do know that he was intent on the company growing bigger than any other shipping company on the East Coast."

"Why, because he was greedy?" Kate asked without thinking.

"Sort of," Michael replied. He moved to the liquor cabinet. "Brandy?" he asked.

"Please," Jake replied for them both.

"He grew up the son of a groom for one of the very rich families in England," Michael explained while he poured. "When he was about sixteen, he left. My grandfather told me his father always said he was just plain tired of waiting on other people. He came to America with every intention of becoming rich and having people wait on him for a change." He paused in his explanation only long enough to hand them each a glass of brandy. "On the trip over, he fell in love with the sea. He took a job on a boat. By the time he was twenty, he had enough money to buy his first vessel. He worked on it himself until he bought the second one. By the time he married in 1891, he had one of the biggest fleets on the coast. He built this house then, for his new wife." Michael's eyes moved about the room on that comment.

"But his true love was the company," Jake muttered knowingly.

Michael absently swirled his brandy around in the glass he held. "And the sea," he added. "At least up until Jacob disappeared." He took a sip. "You haven't told me why you're both so interested in this," he said suddenly, changing the subject.

Kate and Jake looked at each other, not sure exactly what to tell him. "Well, we came upon some information that might explain what happened to Jacob Krinshaw and his fiancée," Jake said slowly.

Michael's brows rose at that. "Really? What information?"

"We can't tell you just yet. Until we get some proof," Jake answered quickly.

The brandy was swirling in Michael's glass again. "I see," he said slowly. "And what kind of proof do you need?"

"We're not sure," Kate put in. "We were hoping you could show us some of Jacob's things."

Michael looked at her hard. Kate got the impression he was trying to look deep enough inside her to actually see her thoughts. "The attic's full of stuff. It seems to be a Krinshaw trait to save everything. It might be valuable someday. But I've been keeping a special box of stuff to show my children. Not that I have any. But then Richard Krinshaw wasn't married until he was nearly forty, so I guess I've got a little time. Marrying late in life also seems to be a Krinshaw trait." He set his glass down. "If you'll excuse me for a moment, I'll get the box."

He left the room, his step hardly making a sound on the wood floor.

"He sounds lonely," Kate whispered once he was gone.

"Yes, he does," Jake replied. His eyes were gazing once again at the portrait of Kaitlan.

Kate sat down, and after a moment Jake did the same.

"You saw something else, didn't you?" He met her eyes only briefly, but he took her hand and held it warmly wrapped within his own.

"It was just a flash, like when Anthony kissed my hand." Her words were whispered. She held his hand tightly and took a sip of her brandy, letting the heat of it wash through her. She felt incredibly comfortable sitting as she was, and she had the vague sensation that she'd sat there before.

Her words still soft, she explained the flash. How she knew she'd interrupted an argument between Richard and Jacob. "For only a second, I saw this room as it was then, Jake," she said. "And it's changed very little."

"I know," he muttered.

Michael returned, carrying a wooden box. He brought it over to the table and sat down on the small sofa across from them. He opened it, saying, "This house is so big, and over the years I've found things. Things that have been tucked away into little hiding places by my relatives and their guests. I found this one day when I was planting in the garden."

He held up a carved, wooden whistle. "Look at what it says on it."

"World's Fair, St. Louis, Missouri, 1904," Jake read.

Michael smiled. "Richard took his wife and sons to St. Louis for the fair. I would imagine that belonged to my grandfather, the younger son."

"Nathaniel," Jake put in.

Michael looked at Jake across the table. "You've certainly done your homework, haven't you?"

Jake only grinned before returning his attention to the articles in the box. There was a pair of gold cuff links. "Where did you find these?"

Kate looked at them, too.

"Those are quite a mystery. I haven't the slightest idea to whom they belonged. I found them in the yellow bedroom at the end of the north wing."

"But that room's always been strictly for unwed lady guests," Kate put in without thinking.

Michael looked at her as he'd looked at Jake before. His gaze now, however, was even sharper. "How did you know that?"

Kate nearly told him she knew because she'd stayed in that room. She managed to clamp her mouth shut before the words could tumble out.

"That's not written anywhere," Michael said, still holding her with his piercing gaze. "No matter how much homework you've done, you couldn't know that. It's just always been that way, like an unwritten law."

Kate couldn't meet his gaze any longer. She knew that they shouldn't try to explain anything to him, but not doing so made her feel like a liar, or something equally bad.

"What exactly is going on here?" Michael asked. His words were even, but his tone was as sharp as his gaze.

"If we could explain it to you, we would," Jake said.

His words took Michael's gaze off Kate and put it on Jake.

"I'd be delighted if you'd try," Michael snapped. "You've come here out of the blue, into my home. And I feel I did the right thing by letting you in, but you refuse to tell me why you're so interested in my family's past. You have the same first names as my ancestors and you know things about my house. She—" he nodded toward Kate "—even looks exactly like my great-uncle's fiancée. And you tell me you can't explain it!" His voice sounded slightly agitated.

"You'd think we were crazy if we told you," Kate said softly.

"I think you're crazy already," he said curtly. His eyes were hard. And for a moment, Kate thought she was looking at Richard Krinshaw when she'd interrupted that argument between him and Jacob. "I must be crazy to sit here with you, sharing personal things regarding my family. But for some strange reason, it just feels right. I feel like I'm supposed to be doing this."

None of them spoke for a while, and the only sound in the room was the crackle of the logs in the fire.

"Please explain this to me," Michael said slowly. "I'm showing you pieces of the Krinshaw family. It's the least you can do."

When neither Jake nor Kate said anything, he pushed on. "I won't think you're crazy, I promise. I just want to know how she could have known about the yellow bedroom."

So they finally told him. In bits and pieces, they told him about the visions and the way they were drawn together by dreams, leaving out what actually occurred in the dreams. Still, Kate was overwhelmed by a rush of warmth just thinking about them. She turned away, thinking that Michael would see her blush if she didn't. But Jake knew her feelings, as she knew he would, and he gave her hand a hard squeeze.

Michael sat and listened to every word, interrupting here and there to ask a question.

"So you think these visions, or whatever they are, are trying to lead you to what happened to Jacob and Kaitlan?" he asked.

Jake gave Kate a knowing look.

"You might as well tell him," she said. "You've told him everything else."

"Tell me what?"

"We already know what happened to them," Jake said.

Michael leaned back slightly. "All right. So what happened to them? Did they really go West like everyone thinks? If they did, Jacob must have given up his art, because I've looked all over the place for any of his paintings. And I haven't found a single piece that bears his signature."

"They were killed." Jake didn't mean to sound so blunt, but he knew of no other way to say it.

"Out West?" Michael's brows rose in surprise.

"No, here. On the Fourth of July, the night they disappeared."

Michael's brows rose even further. "How? By whom?"

Jake went on to explain about the vision where John pushed Jacob over the edge of the cliff. "By a man named John Tallon. Have you ever heard of him?" Jake asked.

"No."

"There's not a John mentioned in any of the old Krinshaw records? A former employee?" Kate asked. She shivered at the sound of his name. Every time she thought of the way he had held her and forced her to kiss him, she felt sick to her stomach.

After a moment's thought, Michael shook his head. "As common as the name is, it doesn't ring any bells. And I don't remember seeing the name Tallon anywhere. But as soon as I get the chance, I'll look through the old books and see if I can find anything." He got up and moved to a small telephone table in the corner of the room. He returned, carrying a small slip of paper and a pen. "Make sure you leave a number where I can reach one of you in case I find something."

Was he looking at Kate when he said that? Jake thought he was. Did Michael want Kate's phone number? Jake felt a surge of unexpected jealousy slide up his spine. He tried to fight it down. He knew he shouldn't feel insecure about Kate, not after the way she'd given herself to him the night before. But he did.

Something in the box on the table caught Kate's eye, and she let go of Jake's hand to reach for it. It took his attention away from his jealousy. She picked up a piece of yellowed parchment. It was folded and threatened to break apart as she unfolded it. She gasped, seeing the words that were written on it.

I'll meeet you at the carousel, my love.

"You found this in the yellow room, too, didn't you?" she asked. Jake leaned over to read the note. Their eyes met in a look of understanding. Michael had to have seen the look, but was kind enough to say nothing.

"Yes," he explained. "When I was about ten, all of the beds in the guest rooms were given new mattresses. I found that tucked down in the frame of the bed before the new mattress was put on."

Kate stared down at the parchment, her heart thudding in her chest. Hardly five hours before, that same note had been written on new parchment with fresh ink. Now it was more than eighty years old and looked it, the parchment yellow and cracking. The only thing that looked the same was the way the words were written, in that curvy, even, precise script. Jacob Krinshaw's handwriting. After a moment, she replaced the note and rested her hand in her lap so Michael could not see how she was shaking. Jake knew. He reached out and grasped her hand again.

"What can you tell us about Kaitlan?" Kate asked, her voice not quite steady, her eyes wandering toward the painting.

Michael's eyes followed Kate's to study the portrait of Kaitlan. "Her last name was McGregor. Jacob met her in a small town down the coast when he went looking for more dock space."

"Port James," Kate put in, the knowledge suddenly coming to her.

"Yes," Michael replied absently. He was still looking at Kaitlan, so he failed to see the look of shock that Kate and Jake were sharing. "Her family was decently well-to-do, and she lived in a big house in the middle of town on Mason Street."

Kate was just surprised with the information. Jake was wondering why they hadn't known it until now.

"Mason Street? I've never heard of it," Kate muttered. Surely Michael could hear the shaking of her voice.

"My grandfather remembered her well," Michael recalled. "And I remember him saying she lived on Mason Street. Number one East Mason Street. He knew her address because she and Jacob wrote each other at least once a week. So he was always seeing her letters in the mail. And Jacob said that she was his number one, as well. My grandfather admired Jacob a great deal and spoke of him often, even in his later years. He spoke of Kaitlan, too, saying she was soft-spoken and smiled almost all the time. People were drawn to her, and he said he didn't know anyone who didn't like her the moment he met her. He remembered that Jacob must have fallen in love at first sight because he talked more about Kaitlan than he did about the docks. She came to visit, by train, three or four times that spring after Jacob asked her to marry him."

Kate was still contemplating Number One Mason Street. She felt she should know where that was, but it just wasn't coming to her.

Michael's eyes moved back to the portrait. "My grandfather also said that Jacob captured her perfectly on canvas. That what you see up there is the true Kaitlan McGregor. I think he was a little in love with her himself, and he didn't marry until his late thirties because he was waiting to find someone like her."

Kate was barely listening. It was driving her mad not knowing Mason Street. Beside her, Jake glanced at his watch, remembering his promise to have her home by early evening.

"We should be going," he said. He really didn't want to leave. He probably could have stayed all night and listened to stories about Jacob and Kaitlan. But the feeling that there was some sort of deadline they had to meet was pressing him more and more. They were running out of time.

He looked at Kate, and it suddenly hit him with the impact of a kick in the stomach. *Kate* was running out of time. Unexplained terror gripped him so hard, he had trouble taking his next breath. He forced a smile at Michael. He felt as though his face might break into pieces.

Kate looked at him, her eyes clearly showing her disappointment. A vision of Kaitlan McGregor flashed through his mind....

Kaitlan McGregor was standing on the platform at the train depot. "Jacob, I don't want to go," she said. Her eyes held that same look of disappointment. She was holding his hand and pressing herself against the side of him.

"I'll always be in your heart, my love," Jacob said softly in her ear. "And I'll be counting the days until next month when I can get down to Port James."

He walked her to the waiting train, hearing the distant call of the conductor. He nearly had to push her onto the train. She kept her eyes glued to him through the windows of the Pullman car as she edged her way down the aisle to find a seat. Finally finding a seat near a window, she pressed her palm against the glass. Her lips mouthed, "I love you."

Jacob blew her a kiss and said the same words, his being out loud.

The train let out a whistle. Steam pulsed out about the cars, and then the train started to move. It picked up speed, leaving the depot. And Jacob Krinshaw watched until it was completely out of sight.

Jake blinked, the vision faded and Michael Krinshaw's drawing room came back into focus. Michael and Kate were talking and hadn't even noticed that Jake was returning from another time, another place.

The visions were always leading them in a certain direction, and Jake wondered about this one. What was it trying to tell him? He looked at Kate. She was still talking and obviously hadn't shared this one with him. He remembered the vision with vivid detail. He remembered the longing that he as Jacob Krinshaw had felt watching the train leave, taking his love away. He'd wanted to go, too, to Kaitlan's house.

And the feeling didn't fade. Jake wanted to go to Kate's house now, to sit in the coziness of her warm kitchen, to sit close to her on the sofa in front of the fire, to crawl next to her under that patchwork quilt on her bed.

"We'd love to come back next weekend and have supper with you, Michael," Kate was saying. "Wouldn't we, Jake?"

"Yes, of course," Jake replied without thinking. He was still dwelling on that vision. Were these visions still trying to tell him something, still pointing him in the direction of Kaitlan McGregor's and Jacob Krinshaw's killer, or were they just bits and pieces of their lives that were coming to him because he was in the Krinshaw house? Or was the last vision really leading him to Kate's house, causing his longing to be there to grow? Jake didn't really know. But he had the feeling that the longer he stayed with Kate, the more he would see and feel of Kaitlan and Jacob's lives together.

He looked again at Kate. She was talking to Michael, something about next Saturday evening at six o'clock. His feeling that she was in danger was growing, too, greatly outweighing his curiosity about Kaitlan and Jacob's life and times in this house.

He stood up, glancing at his watch again. "We really should go," he said, forcing his voice to be even. He was suddenly so afraid for Kate that he could no longer sit. "I promised Kate I'd have her home by early evening, and we have a two-hour drive ahead of us." He was still holding her hand, and his grip tightened. She looked up at him, puzzled by his action. He ignored the look and pulled her to her feet beside him.

"We wanted to visit the Krinshaw Shipping Office, too, remember?" Kate said.

"You'd be wasting your time," Michael put in. "The office is closed on Sundays. If you want to see it, you'll have to come during the week or on Saturday."

"That's too bad," returned Kate. "I was looking forward to seeing it."

"Well, I'd love to show it to you."

Was Michael looking at her with something more than simple friendliness? Or was it Jake's imagination? Or was it a Krinshaw trait to be attracted to anyone resembling Kaitlan McGregor? Was that the danger Jake felt for Kate? Was Michael the danger? Damn, Jake hoped not. He genuinely liked Michael.

He was open and seemed honest, and had taken them into his home when he could have slammed the door in their faces.

Jake gave Michael a hard, intense look, studying the man, trying to look inside him. Michael's eyes were a soft, chocolate brown and hinted of nothing more than simple interest in Jake and Kate. The only other thing about Michael that Jake could clearly see was what Kate had already pointed out—loneliness. Jake guessed the old saying was right; money couldn't buy everything.

Then he saw something else in the way Michael was looking at Kate. He saw love. A love like... like a brother's, he thought, remembering the way his own little brother used to look up to him when they were kids. After all these years, Jake had never forgotten that look of admiration. It was the same look Michael was now giving to Kate. Could he be loving her with that respectful love just as Jacob's brother, Nathaniel, had loved Kaitlan McGregor? The thought seemed to bring all the other thoughts to a screeching halt. And Jake wondered again just how far this thing could go.

Jake was able to tear his staring gaze away when Michael turned to him and offered his hand.

"Well," Michael said, "it's certainly been interesting, to say the least."

Jake chuckled then, thinking there was so much they hadn't even told Michael. Like how Kate and Jake had nearly destroyed Kate's living room during that second lovemaking dream.

"I hope you find out everything you need to know," added Michael.

Terror suddenly tightened around Jake's insides. "I hope so, too," he said, his voice so tight he could barely get the words out. He glanced at Kate.

"You left your phone numbers, didn't you?" Michael asked. "In case I find something."

"Yes," Jake replied, giving Michael's hand a final shake before releasing it. The fear he felt was building, and he was afraid that if he held Michael's hand any longer, his fear would come out into his grip where Michael would feel it. "I left them on the table." He looked back at Kate.

She looked so at ease, he knew she wasn't in tune with him when it came to this terror he was feeling for her. He'd see it in her face if she was. In fact, she was looking more at ease than she had since the first time he'd met her on her porch. She gave him a small smile, and her features softened so that her expression was identical to the expression on Kaitlan McGregor's face in the portrait. Jake sucked in a breath. It was like looking at a ghost.

She let go of his hand to shake Michael's hand, and her face changed. She went back to being just Kate. The Kate from Jake's dreams. The Kate who belonged to him, Jake, and only to him. The Kate whom he wanted to protect. The fear he felt for her was growing, and he was overcome with an overwhelming desire to take her in his arms right then and cradle her against him where she would be safe.

He didn't, of course. He merely took her hand again when she broke loose of Michael's grip.

There was still no rain, but the air was damp and considerably colder when they climbed back into Jake's car. Neither of them said a word, and the only sound in the night was that of Jake starting the engine. Jake slowly drove down the long, tiled drive, and Kate watched the house until it was out of sight.

Still turned away from him, Kate said, "So are you going to tell me what's wrong?"

"Nothing's wrong," he lied. He tried to keep the emotion out of his voice so as not to give himself away, but he failed.

Kate finally turned to face him. Jake could feel her burning gaze, but he refused to take his eyes from the road ahead to meet it. "Oh, right," she replied sarcastically. "Nothing's wrong. The world's just one big, happy place. You keep forgetting how well I can see your thoughts, Jake."

Jake gripped the steering wheel so hard, his knuckles turned white. But he still refused to look at her. She could see inside of him too easily when she looked into his eyes.

"Fine," she said when Jake refused to speak or even look over at her. "I'll figure it out for myself. It might take me a little longer than if you flat out told me, but I've got the next two hours until we get to my house, don't I?"

Jake still said nothing. He wanted to protect her. At least protect her from this fear.

"Let's see," she started. "You were fine when we arrived at Michael's. And I still didn't notice any change in you when he gave you a glass of brandy. But," she said slowly, drawing the word, "you nearly broke my hand when Michael asked us over for supper next weekend."

That was when he'd had the vision, Jake thought. It was just a simple vision of Kaitlan McGregor leaving on the train. So why did it fill him with such terror, such raw terror? He didn't want to tell Kate, at least not until he figured it out. So he let her keep talking.

"You're jealous of him, aren't you?" she asked suddenly.

"Who?" he asked. He'd been thinking of that vision and hadn't really been listening to her.

"Michael," she replied with a frustrated sigh.

"No, I'm not."

"Yes, you are."

"Why would I be jealous of him?" Jake asked. He finally ventured a glance at Kate. His eyes met hers for less than a second. Her gaze told him how sure of herself she was.

For a moment, Jake wondered if it wasn't true. No, he knew for certain Michael didn't want her the way he, himself, wanted her. Then again, wouldn't her ties to the past be stronger to Michael? Jake wondered. Michael was a true Krinshaw, after all. Jake knew he, himself, had no ties at all to anyone named Krinshaw. He knew his family tree all the way back to the Civil War. So why was he playing the part of Jacob Krinshaw and seeing the visions of his life? Why wasn't Michael playing the part? Because Michael is from the line of Jacob's brother, came the answer.

Jake wasn't sure how true that sudden answer was. All he knew for sure was that right now he was feeling terror for Kate McCoy. It was a terror unlike anything he'd ever felt before. And if it meant following her into the bathroom, he was going to do so to protect her. He, Jake, was going to be there for her, not Michael. Michael didn't have the feeling of terror.

Kate's words stopped all his thoughts. "Are you even listening to me?"

"I'm sorry, Kate, what did you say?" He reached over to take her hand again. She clasped his with just as much need.

"I said I think you were jealous because of the way he kept looking at me."

"Maybe I was," Jake admitted. "Just a little at first. But I'm not any more." He wasn't lying. Besides, he didn't have time to be jealous. He'd have to put the fear aside first. Why wasn't Kate feeling it, too? Until now, they'd been linked so closely. "Tell me about that note," he said, changing the subject.

"It was the same one that I found on your pillow this morning, or this afternoon, whenever it was that I woke up," Kate said, her voice taking on an unexpected note of flatness.

Jake noticed it. "What's the matter, Kate?"

"I was just disappointed, that's all," she replied after a moment of remembering how happy she'd felt reading that note, how loved she'd felt.

"Why?"

Kate gave him a small, embarrassed smile, but Jake was looking ahead and didn't see it. "Because I'd thought you'd written it," she explained. She hadn't understood just how easy it was to talk to him until then. She had the feeling there wasn't anything she couldn't tell him.

He squeezed her hand. "I wish I had," he said softly. He wasn't lying. He did wish he had. Or at least he wished he'd known about it. He could have met her at that carousel. She might not have had to face that vision alone. She might not have had to face it at all.

They talked more of their visit with Michael. And they talked of where they felt the visions were leading them. Jake still didn't tell her of his fear for her. They talked the whole way to Kate's house, even talking about what Kate had in her refrigerator for them to eat when they got there.

They didn't know that not too far away, a man sat in a large chair thinking about them, thinking and muttering out loud about what he wanted to do, what he needed to do, to Kate McCoy. He thought of her beauty, of her face. He thought of Kaitlan McGregor, and the two of them blended into one. He thought of the rich, full mouth they shared and he longed to kiss it. He thought of the soft, tawny hair. His fists clenched, his fingers wrapping tightly around the arms of the chair.

Oh, how he wanted to run his hands through that softness before moving his fingers down to her slender throat. Where he wanted to slowly squeeze the life out of her once and for all. He'd killed her before, of course. Three times, as a matter of fact. This time, he'd make sure he did it right. . . .

CHAPTER THIRTEEN

"Take it off," Jake ordered, his voice husky with passion.

Kate's gaze never left his. Slowly she slipped the robe from her shoulders and let it fall to the floor at her feet.

There had been no question that Jake wouldn't stay. In fact, there had been no mention at all of his leaving. They had eaten a light supper of cheese omelets, Jake finishing off the leftover ham. They'd watched television together in front of the fire while Jake helped Kate grade some papers for school the next day. They'd taken another shower together. Jake had climbed into her bed through some unspoken invitation a moment before Kate came out of the bathroom.

Now she stood before him. A shiver passed through her, more from the hot, passionate way he was looking at her than from the cold.

"You are so beautiful," he said under his breath, not even realizing he'd spoken his thoughts out loud.

He saw her blush in the soft light. "No, I'm not."

"Don't argue with me," he replied before he realized they'd spoken the same words in that first dream. He tried to push the dream from his mind. Right then, he wanted nothing to do with any of the dreams. He wanted reality. He wanted the reality of Kate. He wanted no fear, only pleasure.

He pulled back the covers. Kate came to him slowly, her gaze never leaving his. Jake watched the fluid, smooth way she moved, loving every motion. She climbed under the patchwork quilt with him. He wasted no time in taking her in his arms.

She was so soft, so warm, smelling of her own clean scent mixed with that of the soap he'd rubbed on her. There seemed to be no space between their bodies. At first, Jake thought he'd be satisfied just holding her, she was so comfortably wrapped about him. Then she tenderly kissed his throat.

It was a soft, feather-light kiss, and still it shook him, bringing instant fire that seemed to burn up all of his control. He wanted to give her another night like the previous one. He wanted to make love to her whole body, her whole being. He wanted to look into her eyes and see her on the edge of sanity, knowing that his touch would take her over the edge.

And it had been her touch that had done all of those things and more to him. He wanted her now. He needed her immediately, finding it hard to believe that one touch of her lips could wipe away every ounce of control he possessed.

He tangled his fingers in the curls of her hair and pulled her to him, bringing his lips to her in a kiss that tasted so hot, he thought he would surely burn up. And still he couldn't get close enough to her.

"Jake..." She moved her lips from his to utter his name.

"No, honey. No more words," he said, kissing her between each word. "There's no time for words. There's only time to love and taste and feel. Like this." He slipped his hands down the length of her body, while bringing his lips back to hers to give her the taste of his kiss.

But it was the touch of her tongue to his that caused him to shudder. He couldn't wait any longer. He raised himself and slipped inside her, where her warmth surrounded him completely. He heard her gasp and he had no choice but to begin the mating of the souls that was older than time.

"Please, Jake," she cried. "Hold on to me."

"I've got you." He did have her. He held her as tight as he possibly could. It was just so out of control. He was afraid that if he didn't hold on to her, he might fall into some giant black hole, into nothingness. His arms held her, his body possessed her. Her nails dug into his back as though she were holding on to him for life. Maybe she was.

She cried out, and the sound of her voice took him over the edge. In the next second, their bodies touched as never before—lips touching, flesh touching, and souls touching.

And much later as Jake held her close, listening to the soft sounds of her even breathing as she slept, he realized something that was even more earth-shattering than being inside her. He realized he'd fallen in love with her. He finally fell asleep, never letting her go, praying that this fear he had of losing her was groundless. For he knew then that he could never live without her.

Kate woke long before the alarm went off.

Oh, she thought again, how wonderful it felt to be close to him. He smelled good. His skin was soft and warm like comfortable leather, and it seemed to call out for her touch.

She pressed up against the warmth of Jake, his arm holding her against him, her head resting where his upper chest met his lower shoulder. And the soft, dark fuzz there tickled her cheek.

It was a wonderful feeling to wake up beside him. Kate smiled, relishing that wonderful feeling. The gray light of the morning was trying to push through the windows, and Kate closed her eyes against it. She didn't want morning to come. She didn't want to move.

She didn't realize Jake was awake until his fingers touched her hair.

"Good morning," she said softly. She opened her eyes, taking in the vision of his dark, muscled chest.

"Good morning to you." His voice was husky, deep, sounding a lot like it had when he was making love to her. He kissed the top of her head.

Kate ran her fingers over his chest, moved them slowly down his tight, flat stomach.

His free hand covered hers and stopped its movement. "If you keep that up, Kate, you'll be walking funny in front of your students."

Kate giggled like a schoolgirl at the thought and pulled her hand free to continue. With strength and a quickness that surprised her, he rolled her onto her back, his weight comfortably on her.

"You asked for it," he muttered before his lips came down on hers. He became a part of her so easily, so fully, with so much warmth. The last thing on Kate's mind was if she was going to have trouble walking later.

And later, she was too busy having trouble getting to work on time to think about having trouble walking. Jake laughed at her and fixed coffee, handing her a cup of the warm brew while she was in the bathroom trying to get her curls under some sort of control. She threw down the brush with a sigh.

Jake stood at the door, watching her, forcing himself to smile. That fear for her was back in full force. He didn't want her to go to work. He didn't want her out of his sight.

He watched her dress. Again he wanted her, but the desire didn't override the terror he felt for her as it had the night before. It was because the fear was stronger now. And he wouldn't have thought that possible. He'd thought and hoped that he wouldn't be so afraid for her while here in her house with her. He didn't even know why there was such fear for her. It was just there. And stronger than ever. It was as though a little voice inside his head were telling him that if he let her go to work, he'd never see her again. Something was going to happen. And it was going to happen today.

"Stay home, Kate," he said behind her. His throat was so tight with his fear for her, he could barely speak.

Kate looked at him in the mirror. She misread the fear in his voice for passion, and she grinned at him. A slight blush even rose in her cheeks.

"What's the matter, big boy?" she asked, her eyes never leaving his in the mirror. "Haven't you had enough?" The color in her cheeks deepened with her own words.

Jake was quiet for a long moment. He wanted to lie to her. Well, it wouldn't actually be a lie. He did want her again. If he pushed the fear from his mind and let himself go, he could lay her down right here on the bathroom tile. But he knew that making love to her would only allow him to forget his fear for a short time. After his passion was spent, his fear would return even stronger than before.

No, it was time to tell her the truth.

"Kate," he said slowly. "I have this terrible fear that something's going to happen to you today. Call it a premonition. Call it whatever you like. But I want you to stay with me so I can protect you."

"Have you had another vision you haven't told me about?" she asked.

"No," he lied, still hiding the vision of the train depot from her. "It's just a feeling I have. And it won't go away. It just keeps getting stronger."

"And you think I need your protection?"

Hell, he could suddenly see that she was playing with him, not taking anything he was saying seriously. "Yes." He gritted his teeth to keep from yelling at her.

"Well—" she went back to her makeup routine "—I have to admit that when this first started, I was really afraid. But since we've found out who the killer is, I don't feel that fear any longer. So I don't need your protection, Jake." She turned her attention back to the mirror to apply some blush. "I can take care of myself. And it's only a school, for crying out loud. I'll be perfectly safe there." Her voice was steady, and she sounded completely convinced with her words.

Jake, on the other hand, was not convinced.

He drew closer and set her coffee cup on the counter. "Come on, Kate," he said. He held her shoulders in his strong hands. "Call in, just for today, and stay here with me."

Kate's grin returned. "You just want me to stay in bed with you."

If it kept her here, fine, Jake thought. "I admit it would be a wonderful way to spend the day." He leaned down and kissed her throat. She felt so warm and wonderfully alive to his lips. The tile on the bathroom floor was looking more and more inviting.

She smiled and moaned at his touch and moved her head, giving him greater access to her tender throat. Her blush brush dropped to the counter with a loud clank, and for several long seconds, Jake thought she might take him up on his suggestion and call in sick.

In the end, she didn't. "I have to go," she said, hardly moving out of reach of his lips.

Jake groaned and contemplated tying her up to keep her there. Even though he knew he couldn't. He knew he'd never force her into doing anything she didn't want to do. If he did, he would be sinking to the same level as John Tallon, who tried to force himself on Kaitlan McGregor. Jake knew all he could really do was stay as close to her as he could and protect her when the time came. And he wasn't even totally sure that the time would even come.

"At least let me drive you to work," he whispered in her ear.

"All right," she agreed.

She turned from him to go back into the bedroom. He followed.

"And let me pick you up at lunchtime. When is it?" he added.

"From ten minutes to twelve to ten minutes to one."

She headed out of the room and down the hall to the stairs. Jake followed. At the door, Kate reached for her coat as she glanced at her watch. "We need to leave now, or I really will be late."

"What will you do while I'm gone?" she asked once they were settled in his car, on their way to the grade school.

Jake didn't need to ask where it was—he already seemed to know. He shrugged absently at her question. "I don't know. I thought I might go to the library and see what information I can get on Kaitlan McGregor."

"Port James doesn't have a public library," Kate informed him. She was watching him intently from across the car. It was so nice having him with her. It was nice having someone to share thoughts and feelings and mornings with. It was nice of him to take her to work.

Then a whole group of questions popped into her mind with such intensity that she felt she'd been kicked in the stomach.

Yeah, but how long will it last? And even if it does last, will it be one of those long-distance relationships? Is that what you want? And if you really think about it, he's gotten pretty personal doing things like spending the night in your bed, making your coffee, watching you in the bathroom. Do you think it's safe having him that close?

Jake glanced over to find her blinking at him just as she had the first time she'd found him on her porch, as if she couldn't believe that she was actually looking at him.

In that same instant, her thoughts and fears came to him in one giant wave of telepathy. He took one hand from the wheel to grasp hers. That simple tender action seemed to calm her slightly. He could actually feel the tightness leave her hand.

"Kate?"

His voice was soft, not too different from the seductive tone he used when they were making love. It just lacked the huskiness.

"Yes, Jake?"

She was staring at him. Jake could feel her eyes. He couldn't meet them because he had to keep his on the road.

"You've trusted me with your body. Don't you think it's time you trusted me with everything else?" He raised her hand and kissed the back of it.

"Can I, Jake?" she asked slowly.

He was disappointed to see they had reached the school. He thought of driving around the block so he would have more time to convince her, but she was late already. He'd have to wait until lunch hour. He stopped in the parking lot to let her out, but he wasn't quite ready to release her hand. He turned and met her gaze fully.

What he saw terrified him. She was in his arms, but limp, lifeless. He was cradling her, calling her name, trying to call her back to him.

Dear God!

He blinked away the vision, his blood turning cold with dread that sent shivers up his spine and caused his hair to stand up on the back of his neck. He coughed, feeling he might choke, and he swallowed down the sick taste of fear in his mouth, trying to keep it hidden from her.

"You can trust me, Kate," he said slowly, his voice sounding harsh because his throat was so tight. He could hardly breathe.

She could see in his eyes that there was more he wasn't telling her, but she could also see that what he said was true. And she wanted to believe it. She wanted to trust him. And she realized she wanted more from him. But she kept that to herself. She was holding her free hand to her chest. Instead of feeling her heart's usual *lub-dub, lub-dub,* she thought it was saying something more like *tell him, tell him.* Tell him how you feel.

But she didn't. She couldn't. Not yet. Telling him would put her in a very vulnerable position. A position where she wasn't ready to be just yet, no matter how much she trusted him.

"I have to go," she said slowly, suddenly wishing she'd taken him up on his suggestion and called in sick. She felt they needed to stay together. She was feeling that strongly right now.

In the distance, the school bell rang. Kate reached for the door handle, but Jake's squeeze of her hand held her in her place. He leaned across the seat and his lips settled on hers with soft, familiar excitement. His tongue brushed against hers in a soft, even caress. Before she could even relish the feeling, he pulled away, leaving her lips tingling and crying out for more.

"I'll be here to pick you up for lunch."

Kate only nodded, afraid of how her voice would sound if she tried to speak. She climbed out of the car, leaning down to look in the window at him. "Even though there isn't a public library," she said, her voice sounding only slightly shaky from that kiss, "there is the Port James Historical Society. It's in a building down on West Main Street. You can't miss it. There's a big sign out front."

Her gaze held his. He was reluctant to leave, and she suddenly didn't want him to go. Together all weekend, she felt they'd had a certain strength. Once she walked away and entered the school, surrounded by children or not, she'd be on her own. She wondered if she would be strong enough should something happen. What if she had another vision while she was writing sentences on the blackboard for the children to copy? She swallowed hard, feeling the first pangs of fear tighten in her stomach. She really had no choice. Others, children and fellow teachers alike, had already seen her in the parking lot. Some had actually stopped to look, trying to see whom she was with, even though Kate had ignored the looks.

"Thanks," he muttered.

Kate tried to smile.

And the smile he offered in return looked just as forced.

Trying not to think about it, she slammed the door and walked toward the building, fighting the urge to turn and wave at the very least. She entered the building, not even noticing the clean, waxed smell of the halls that were now so familiar to her. Inside the door, she finally gave in to the urge to look back at him.

"Yes, I trust you," she whispered to herself. "But what about love?" With a sigh, she turned and headed down the hall. She entered her class to find her students lined up against the windows. Because the building was shaped like an L and the parking lot located on the inside of that L, her students had been able to see her.

She stepped into the room, and they all turned to look at her. "I am sorry I'm late," she apologized.

They were watching her with wide, curious eyes.

"Let's take our seats, children. It's time to begin." She was trying desperately to ignore their looks.

Reluctantly, they made their way to their small desks.

"He kissed you," Melanie Webster said with exasperated courage.

"Yes," Kate said, brushing it off, hoping she didn't blush in the meantime.

"Are you going to marry him?" asked Jimmy Salem.

Kate sighed. Oh, it promised to be another exciting day!

The children kept her so busy, she didn't realize lunchtime had arrived until the bell rang. She lined them up and led them to the lunchroom. Knowing they were safe in the hands of a fellow teacher, Mrs. Weatherby, who was filling in for her at cafeteria duty and then playground duty, Kate took her leave. Jake was waiting for her at the curb in the loading zone.

"Hi," she said, climbing in. She nearly giggled. The way he was treating her made her feel young again. She had pushed her fears of this relationship aside long before the morning ended. She had faced the fact that she didn't know how long it would last and decided to enjoy every minute of it and stop worrying about what might come in the end.

But one look at Jake's face nearly wiped the smile she was wearing for him right off her face.

"What is it?" she asked, her voice filling with alarm. "What's the matter? Something's happened, hasn't it?"

"Let's go have lunch," he said, his voice sounding oddly flat. "Then we'll talk."

Kate refused to be put off. That he would even try to do so surprised her, after all they'd been through together. "Let's talk now," she said. "You learned something, didn't you, something we didn't know before."

"Yes." A lot, he nearly added. More than he'd ever expected to learn. He didn't look at her when he replied. He looked at the road ahead. He knew if she saw his eyes, she'd see the terror he was feeling.

"So tell me," she pushed. She reached over to rest her hand on his leg as he drove.

Hell, he didn't even know where to begin.

"I spent most of the morning at the Historical Society."

"Was there something regarding Kaitlan McGregor?" Kate questioned. She was eager to know about this woman who had invaded her dreams.

Jake was driving back to Kate's house. "Quite a bit, actually. There was only Kaitlan and her father. His name was Winston. He was the mayor of Port James for many years. After Kaitlan disappeared, he never believed that she and Jacob had run off together and gone West. He hired investigators to find her, but they failed. After two years he accepted the fact that she might be dead. But I guess he couldn't handle the thought of never finding his daughter. He got really sick and died in the winter of 1913. There was no other family. And the house and all its contents were sold the following spring."

"It wasn't auctioned?" Kate asked.

"No. There wasn't any need to auction it. McGregor was a careful man and good with finances. He had secured his own future and his daughter's as well. He had plenty of money and very few debts. The only reason it was sold at all was because a buyer was interested."

They reached Kate's street. "So where was this house? Does it still exist?" she asked, paying more attention to what Jake was telling her than to where they were.

"The name of Mason Street was changed in 1930 to honor two of Port James's mayors. One was McGregor and the other was Gates Hall who was mayor from 1918 to 1924. It became Wins-Gate Drive."

Jake could feel Kate's gaze burning him with its intensity. He pulled into her drive and stopped, killing the engine and finally turning to face her. He could see from the look of shock on her face that his words were finally sinking in.

"And later the spelling was changed, right?" she asked, her voice no more than a whisper. "To Windsgate?"

"Yes."

"One East Windsgate Drive," Kate muttered. She turned her head slowly, her eyes leaving his, to look at the house, at that address, to stare at it. "I'm living in Kaitlan's house."

"Yes," he said again. "And sleeping in what was her room."

Kate climbed out of the car slowly, her eyes glued to the house she'd called home for more than a year. "Why didn't we know it, Jake?" she asked. "We knew so many other things."

"I don't know," he answered honestly, coming around the car to take her hand. There was still so much more he had to tell her, so much he didn't want to tell her. He forced a smile at her when she finally looked back at him. "I fixed sautéed beef sandwiches for lunch."

The smile she returned to him was very small, hardly visible actually. "That sounds great," she lied. Suddenly eating was the last thing on her list of things to do.

Jake let go of her hand, but held her close with his arm around her shoulder. "You know the strangest thing, Kate?"

"What?"

They walked slowly toward the front porch.

"I had a vision last night of Kaitlan when she left Willows Point on a train."

"Why didn't you tell me before?"

He shrugged absently as though the fear meant nothing. "I don't know. It didn't seem all that important. But I distinctly remember this silver brooch she wore. It was carved, very detailed, in the shape of a rose. I saw it in the Historical Society. I held it. It's old and tarnished now. And yet it felt so warm when it was in my hand. I expected something more to come, but nothing did."

They climbed the porch steps slowly. A memory came to Kate. "It took her several hours to get home by train," Kate said, as though she herself had been the one who'd made the trip, and the memory was her own. "She walked home from the depot because there was no one there to meet her. They had three servants, a housekeeper, a cook and a carriage driver. She had to send the carriage driver back to fetch her luggage."

Kate could clearly see Kaitlan McGregor climbing the steps and entering the house on that warm spring day in May. She could see the determination in Kaitlan's step and the way she gracefully peeled her gloves off just before she went through the front door. She was looking for her father to ask him why he wasn't at the depot to meet her.

Kate and Jake now entered through that same front door, and the lingering aroma of beef touched Kate. It brought to the surface what little appetite she had left. They went to the kitchen where Jake had lunch waiting and set out on the table. That single rose he had given her, wilting though it was, served as a centerpiece.

They sat down, and Kate, moving automatically, went about fixing her sandwich.

"There's more, isn't there?" she asked. She set her sandwich on the plate before her, afraid to take a single bite. She was afraid that if she did eat, whatever more Jake had to tell her just might make her lose it. The look in his eyes told her it was bad, and she wasn't even sure she wanted to hear it.

"Yes," he replied.

His eyes shifted and looked down at the sandwich he was making for himself, refusing to look at her.

"About Kaitlan McGregor or her father?" Kate pushed.

He finally met her gaze, and Kate fought down a shiver at the fear she saw in his eyes.

"No." His Adam's apple moved with a hard swallow.

"Then what is it?" Her fear was turning into something not too far from anger. And she welcomed it. Anger was much easier to handle than fear.

"Over the years, the house has been sold and resold, owned and occupied by various families."

Kate was staring at him across the table. "That's what I would expect, Jake."

He took a bite of his sandwich and chewed it slowly. The fact that he was taking so long to tell her was just giving her anger more time to fully flourish.

"And," he finally went on, "there were two owners who were, as you might say, different from the others."

"Different, how?" Kate's lunch sat growing cold in front of her, now fully forgotten.

"They were both young, single women," Jake said.

Kate leaned on the table, her elbows on either side of her plate. "So what makes that different?"

Jake shrugged. "Nothing really. Except the first one, in 1931, was named Katherine McWilliams. And everyone called her Katie."

"Really?" Kate felt her own eyes widen.

"Yes. Then in 1954, Miss Katrine Macke bought the house."

Kate forced herself to blink and then to take a breath. "Don't tell me, everyone called her Kate, too."

"That's right. And they were both schoolteachers."

Kate was suddenly cold. She took her elbows from the table to cross her arms in front of her in an attempt to ward off the cold. The tiny hairs on the back of her neck were standing up, and she fought the urge to reach back and scratch them.

"And now I'm living here and I'm teaching and I actually bear the name of the first Kaitlan, not just something close to it." Her words came out slowly, each one sounding heavily weighted. "Where does it put me?" she asked, just as slowly. "What happened to the other two?"

Jake took a long time in replying. Just when Kate thought she might have to throw her plate at him in frustration, he said, "They disappeared, Kate."

CHAPTER FOURTEEN

Kate stared at Jake in wide-eyed shock.

"Disappeared?" she echoed.

Jake nodded.

Kate didn't believe it. Her mind simply refused to accept it. "And no one ever found them?"

"No," he said simply. It appeared his sandwich was now forgotten, too.

"Did anyone ever look for them?" Kate asked, her voice rising. But with fear or anger, she wasn't sure.

"Yes," Jake said. He never took his eyes from her. He felt the need to touch her, but her arms were still folded tightly across her chest. So he got up and moved around the table behind her. He placed his hands on her shoulders, offering what comfort he could, and leaned down to press his cheek to hers. It was a rather uncomfortable position, but he endured it for a moment before grasping her shoulders tighter, nearly pulling her right out of the chair so he could hold her in his arms.

She melted into his embrace. "Who looked for them, Jake?" she whispered against his chest. His heart was beating strong and loud. She could hear it and feel it just below her chin. She turned her head, pressing her ear to his chest. His chin rested lightly on top of her head. She heard his lungs fill with air. He felt so strong, so real, so with her. He was what she needed.

"The police, and then private investigators hired by their families. Both women had relatives who wanted them found."

"And they never were?"

"Not a trace."

The room was quiet for a long moment. Jake kept her wrapped tightly in his arms. He didn't tell her, but it was the only place he felt she was safe.

What he didn't know was that she felt that way, too.

"I don't want to join them, Jake," she said, her voice shaking slightly.

"I won't let you," he said. He didn't know how it sounded to her, but he meant it. He had looked for her all his life. And now that he'd found her, he wasn't about to let her go. "I want you to call in to work, Kate. Tell them you won't be back today."

Against his chest, she shook her head. "I can't do that. Too many people saw me leave with you. They'd never believe I was sick. Besides, it's too late to find a substitute for my class. I have to go back."

Reluctantly, Jake finally agreed. "All right. But only if you let me drive you back and pick you up at the end of the day. Promise you'll wait for me."

She promised, but her words were muffled against his shirt.

Jake never let her go. He held her close until he was forced to return her to the little people who depended on her for their first-grade education.

"Four o'clock," he said before he let her get out of the car in the parking lot.

"I'll be here," she promised.

He kissed her one last time and watched her get out. This time, she turned at the entrance of the building and waved to him.

Jake held up one hand in return and was filled with the sudden, terrifying thought that this was going to be the last time he ever saw her. He gripped the steering wheel to keep from shaking and watched her until she was gone. Then he stared at the building for a long time, wondering again if his fear for Kate and the disappearances of the other two women had something to do with the school. All three were teachers, after all. He'd pondered over that question ever since he'd learned at the Historical Society about the other two Kates. At least until he'd learned that the school building before him wasn't built until 1959. So neither of the other two women had taught at that facility. And the second one, Katrine Macke, disappeared in August of 1956. School wouldn't even have been in session then.

No, Jake told himself again. The danger had nothing to do with the school. He was nearly convinced of that. He felt that if it did have something to do with the school, the visions would have led them there. So for now, he tried to breathe a little easier and convince himself that Kate was safe while she was there.

He finally started the car and pulled slowly out of the parking lot. He glanced at his watch. Only three hours before he picked her up again. It wouldn't be easy, but he could wait that long. She'd be safe for that long without him, wouldn't she? Of course she would. He worked to convince himself of that all the way back to her house.

And for Kate back at the school, teaching her children with a bubbling smile—to keep from letting them know the fear she felt—was the hardest thing she'd ever had to do. Every sudden noise caused her to jump and her heart to slam in her chest. By the end of the day, she was a nervous wreck and her empty stomach felt like it was tied in knots.

The children were dismissed at 3:25, which gave Kate thirty-five minutes to set the room straight for the next day.

She had bent over to retrieve a toy that had been left out when a voice startled her. "I see you found a guy all on your own."

The unexpected sound caused Kate to look up with a start, bumping her head on a nearby desk. Just inside the doorway was her friend Maddie Jackson.

"Sorry," said Maddie, stepping farther into the room. "I didn't mean to scare you."

Kate looked at her with wide eyes for a moment before forcing herself to relax.

"I really did scare you, didn't I?" Maddie came even closer. "You're as white as a ghost."

Wonderful choice of words, Kate thought. "Thanks a lot," she replied sarcastically. She felt all she'd done since lunch was walk a tightrope.

"You must have had a bad day," Maddie muttered. "And he even picked you up for lunch. What happened, did you have a fight over a Caesar salad or something?"

Kate answered the question with "Nothing happened." It was simple and direct, and it was about all she could deliver at the moment. Talking about the visions and how she'd spent the weekend required thinking about them. And if she allowed herself to think about them, she'd only be dredging up the fear she'd fought to push aside all afternoon. She just didn't need it. She finished picking up toys, keeping herself busy enough so she didn't think about living in Kaitlan McGregor's house or wonder what happened to the other two teachers. Or worse, wonder if the same fate was going to happen to her.

"So when do I get to meet him?" Maddie asked. She half sat and half leaned on top of one of the small desks.

Kate sighed heavily, thinking now was a bad time to expand her social life. "How about next weekend?" she replied, trying to keep her voice light, hoping that Maddie would assume her rotten attitude was caused by a class of rowdy first-graders.

"That sounds great. The four of us could grab a bite somewhere and then maybe take in a movie. Gabe and I haven't been to a movie in months." Maddie's voice was full of anticipation and laughter.

Kate smiled. "That sounds like fun," she said, despite her dark thought that it would be fun provided she was still alive.

Maddie's face turned serious, even though her eyes were still sparkling with happiness. Kate thought they must be quite a contrast to her own, which had to be reflecting the terror she felt at the thought of possibly not being alive on Saturday night.

"What's his name, anyway?" Maddie asked. "Or are you not going to tell me in an effort to keep him all to yourself?"

"Jake. Jake Casperson," replied Kate as she finished clearing off her desk. She had tried most of the afternoon to stay as organized as possible, and her work had paid off. She had no papers to take home and grade, and the next day's work was ready to be handed out.

"How'd you meet him?" Maddie asked.

Any other time, Kate probably would have welcomed that kind of good-humored questioning. But that last question put her on the spot. How could she answer it? By telling Maddie she and Jake had met in their dreams? Maddie would laugh all the way home. "We sort of bumped into each other," Kate finally replied after thinking about it. She suddenly felt exhausted from being on an emotional roller coaster.

She rubbed her neck absently and wondered if Jake would be good enough to fix her supper as he had lunch. She would have liked nothing better than another nice bath, an easy supper and to lie in Jake's arms and sleep for about ten or twelve hours.

"And I assume you spent most of the weekend with him, didn't you?" came Maddie's next question.

She was a regular little investigative reporter today, Kate thought. "Why would you assume that?" she asked.

"Because I called you to see if you wanted to hit an auction Sunday, but there was no answer."

"Did you find anything good at the auction?" Kate asked, purposely changing the subject.

Maddie shook her head. "No. It was a real waste. I'm sure wherever you were and whatever you were doing were much more fun."

Kate thought of the vision that had taken her from the carousel house to the village park. Don't be too sure of that, Maddie, she nearly said before she forcefully clamped her mouth shut.

"Kate?"

Kate turned sharply toward the door at the sound of Jake's voice, and Maddie nearly slipped off the desk in her own effort to turn. Kate wanted to laugh, seeing Maddie's eyes widen as she took in Jake's stocky build and sunny good looks. Kate just smiled, and for the first time all day, the smile wasn't forced.

"I know I'm a little early, but I was hoping you might be ready to go," Jake said after Kate introduced him to Maddie. The truth was, he had worried about Kate all afternoon, and almost hadn't been able to wait until three-thirty. He certainly couldn't have waited until four.

"Well, I'll leave you two alone," said Maddie, excusing herself. "It was sure nice to meet you, Jake. Don't forget about this weekend, Kate." The way Maddie was beaming, it was evident she approved of Jake. Then she was gone, disappearing out the door. Her tap of her heels echoed down the hall for a moment until it could be heard no longer.

"This weekend?" Jake questioned.

"Oh, she asked if the four of us wanted to get together," Kate replied absently. She picked up her bag. She was so glad to see Jake that it took her a moment to remember.

"What about dinner with Michael?" he reminded her.

"Oh, I forgot," she muttered. "I'll talk to her about it later. Besides, we didn't make any definite plans."

"We'll worry about it later, after all of this is over," said Jake, stepping closer to her. He simply didn't have room to worry over a filled social calendar. He was too busy worrying about Kate.

She offered him a small smile. "And if something happens to me, we won't have to worry about it at all, will we?"

He took her hands, warming them in his own. "I'm not going to let anything happen to you, Kate."

Kate didn't know how to reply. She wanted to believe his words. But the truth was, anything could happen. Because Kate had no control within the visions, there was no predicting what could happen. What if she stepped out in front of a car while she was under the spell of a vision?

"She sounds like a happy, fun person," said Jake, glancing at the door where Maddie had gone only moments before. His words brought her thoughts back to the present.

"She is," agreed Kate. "And for a while, she made me feel, well, normal again." There was no other word Kate could think to describe the feeling that life was as it should be, the way it had been before the dreams and the fear. She thought of the look on Maddie's face when she looked at Jake, and she nearly laughed again.

"Are you ready?" Jake asked.

She was ready to leave, she thought. But she had no idea how ready she was to face whatever might be ahead for her.

They held hands, walking to the parking lot.

"Any visions?" he asked softly.

"No, nothing. You?"

"No, thank God."

They reached his car, and he opened the door for her. Kate let go of him only long enough to get in.

"I hope you don't mind that I went to the grocery store and got some things for supper," Jake said, climbing in. "You didn't have much in the house." Besides, it had given him something to do. Something to keep his mind on instead of worrying about Kate. Seeing her, having her close to him, holding her hand, brought such a feeling of relief at knowing she was safe. It wasn't quite enough to erase the fear Jake had for her, but it did give him hope that she might get through this unharmed.

They ate a delicious supper of stew Jake had prepared and crusty bread. The food filled Kate with much-needed warmth and seemed to ease the knots in her stomach.

Then they moved into Kate's living room where they curled up together on the sofa with steaming cups of tea nearby and a fire blazing in the fireplace. Between them, there was an unspoken need to touch and be touched. Touching warmed them more than the tea or the stew ever could. Their lips touched, not with quite the urgency they sometimes did when they made love, but with a simple need to feel and be felt. Hands and fingers did their own warming, exploring and feeling. It was an experience Kate had never known before.

Being touched, caressed and massaged so slowly, feeling the heat of Jake's hands, fingers and the rest of his body, pressed against hers, made Kate light-headed. They said little. As with the previous night, there was simply no room for words. They were communicating in a delicate way, the way of touch and feel. It was as though their bodies knew just what they needed to erase the tension, the fear that had come with the day, and they were responding to that need.

At least Kate knew she was responding. The fear was easing. Everything was easing. She felt almost as if she'd had a little too much wine. But this was much better than any alcoholic buzz. This was something she knew wasn't going to give her a headache. She thought Jake was responding as well. Beneath her fingers, she could feel the tension easing from his body. It gave her a wonderful sense of power and control over him. And the way he was touching her left her with a wonderful feeling of floating in the clouds.

"This feels so good, Jake," she whispered. Even her whisper sounded loud in the room. "I can't remember the last time I felt so good."

"What about this morning when I made love to you?"

Kate smiled at the memory. "That felt good, too, just different."

"Do you want to feel that good again?" he asked.

Kate's smile grew, and there was no forcefulness in it. "Only if you promise not to stop touching me like you are."

"I'll never stop touching you, Kate, never," he promised.

Jake took her to the end of the earth. And when they finally returned, tumbling back into reality, Kate felt elated, and safe, and happy. The fear was gone.

"Thank you," she whispered again.

Still holding her, he chuckled tenderly. "You're quite welcome."

"Not only for what you just did, but for taking away my fear. It feels so good not to have it." She clung to him, refusing to let go of his warmth, refusing to let the fear return to her. "And I guess you were wrong about something happening to me today. Not that I'm disappointed, of course."

Jake's reply was a simple, soft kiss to her lips. He still felt fear for her, and he didn't want to spoil her good feeling by telling her.

They talked more, still holding each other. The words themselves meant little, though. He told her of his afternoon, how he'd enjoyed cooking in her kitchen, how he'd looked forward to her coming home after work.

"By the way, I called Anthony," Jake said softly. "I hope you don't mind. I just thought it might be a good idea to let him know where I am in case he needs me for something."

Kate smiled, watching the fire. "Of course I don't mind. I think it's a good idea. How's he doing?"

"Fine, I think. Busier than ever by the sound of things. I never even asked you about your day," Jake added. "How were your kids?"

Kate's smile continued as she thought of them. "About the usual," she replied. "It always amazes me how eager they are at that age. They're eager to learn, eager to play, eager for attention, eager for anything and everything."

Jake watched her while she talked about her students, and he noticed the brightness that came over her eyes. He thought she deserved children of her own, perhaps even *needed* children of her own. He thought he could sense just how much she wanted them. He could see himself giving them to her, and a happy, content feeling washed over him at the thought of forming a family with her. Would their children be blonde, with his brown eyes or her green eyes? He settled down with her pressing against him, as close as she could. Not only would the sofa allow for little room, but both of them needed the closeness, the warmth.

He felt her relaxing and knew she was drifting off to sleep. He continued to think about a family with her, hoping those thoughts would keep the fear for her from growing, at least for now. He'd thought and hoped he'd succeeded in doing that. Until her screams woke him.

* * *

Kate drifted into the nothingness of sleep with a feeling of contentment, safety and warmth that she'd never known before.

She woke some time later to darkness. And there was something on her, something heavy. She tried to move and found it nearly impossible. Had she and Jake turned around on the sofa? she wondered. Was he now lying right on top of her? It didn't feel like him, and it didn't smell like him. Although the weight did feel evenly distributed, it smelled musty and dirty—what little of it she could smell. It was hard for her to breathe.

She was cold. Whatever was on top of her was cold and damp. She shivered.

She was finally able to get one of her arms out from beneath the heavy weight. She moved it around, feeling something rain down, hitting her, putting more heaviness on her. Her hand touched what was on her, what was around her everywhere. And the knowledge of what was happening to her registered in her mind like the flash of a bolt of lightning.

Terror passed through her so strongly that her stomach twisted and she thought she might be sick. She swallowed hard. She absolutely could not be sick. Not now, not while she was trapped. She felt the raining of more weight on her.

More earth. She was being buried. Buried alive...

She tried to scream, but cold, black dirt fell into her mouth, choking her. And there wasn't even room to turn her head and spit it out.

She fought desperately to free her other arm, to free herself. If she didn't, she was going to die. And soon. Because there was no more air to breathe. Even if there was, she couldn't breathe past the dirt clogging her throat.

And somewhere in the distance, she heard a voice.

"It will be over soon, Kaitlan, sweet Kaitlan. I promise."

She heard the voice, but didn't concentrate on it. She was too busy concentrating on reaching the air again. Already she was having trouble holding her eyes open....

"Kate!" Jake shook her, trying to wake her. "Kate!" She was still screaming, still refusing to wake up. Her arm swung wildly, and before Jake could grab her wrist, she cuffed him on the ear. Pain registered in his head, but he ignored it.

She gasped for air, and it frightened him. Why the hell couldn't he wake her?

"Kate, wake up! It's just a dream!" he yelled, his face only inches from hers. Then he felt an incredible urge to laugh at his own words, remembering all the dreams he and Kate had shared. And he might have laughed, had Kate not been screaming as she was.

He shook her one last time, and her eyes popped open. It was another few seconds before those green eyes focused on him, though. She sucked in what seemed like huge gulps of air.

"Kate?" he asked, his voice softening several decibels.

"Jake? Oh, Jake," she whispered. She was now panting and sobbing, her tears sliding down her cheeks one after another. She grabbed him and held on to him tighter than she ever had before.

Jake held her, giving her what little comfort came from it. He could feel her shaking beneath him. She was cold, and he covered her with his body, offering her his warmth. "It's all right," he said. "It's all over." He said those words for his own benefit as well as hers. She'd scared the hell out of him. He lightly kissed her cheek, and he tasted the salt of her tears.

"Oh, Jake, I was being buried alive," she explained through her sobs. "Someone was shoveling dirt on me. It was so cold and smelly. I tried to scream, but dirt fell into my mouth. And I couldn't get out."

"It's all right, Kate," he tried to reassure her. He was really trying to reassure himself. If it fit into the pattern of the rest of their dreams, then it could be true in some way, either by happening to Kate in the future or by being what had already happened to someone else, perhaps one of the other two Kates who'd disappeared. Either way, it scared the hell out of him. And he was doing his best not to let her know how he was feeling.

He slipped away from her and got off the sofa.

"Where are you going?" she asked, her voice filling with alarm. She clutched his arm, trying to hold him in place.

"I'm taking you to bed." He moved just enough to lift her into his arms. As though she weighed nothing, he carried her up the stairs to her room. He moved through the darkness like a cat, knowing her house as though he'd lived in it forever. He placed her gently on her patchwork quilt. He reached around her and pulled the other end of it back so she could climb under. And he tucked it around her as if she were a child. Then he turned back to the door.

"Now where are you going?" she asked again.

"I'll be right back," he promised. "I have to check the fire and make sure it's out."

He left before Kate could stop him. She snuggled down under the quilts on her bed, trying to warm up, feeling that she never would. She closed her eyes for a moment, trying to relax, but the memory of her dream returned with the darkness. Her room was dark, too, but held a sense of familiarity. She recognized its smell and could see the dark shapes of the furniture. And because there was nothing frightening about it, when she kept her eyes open.

She waited for Jake. She felt she'd been waiting forever. When she was finally about to call him, he came back. He turned on the small lamp beside her bed. Although its light was soft, the sudden change caused Kate to blink several times before she was used to it.

Jake held out a mug to her. "The fire's fine," he said. "I also checked all the doors downstairs and the windows, and I heated up some milk for you. I thought it might settle you and help you sleep."

Kate offered him a smile, just a small one. She reached to take the mug, and her hand was shaking. She did her best to force it still. The shaking didn't quite stop, but it stilled enough that she didn't spill her milk. The milk wasn't hot, just comfortably warm, and Kate took a deep, long swallow, letting the heat of the milk spread inside her.

"Do you want to tell me about it?" Jake reached one hand out to rest it on her leg under the covers.

"There's not much more to tell. I couldn't breathe. I couldn't see. I couldn't move. It was horrible." She shivered thinking about it, and a few drops of milk sloshed out of the cup to land on the quilt where it was pressed up against Kate's chest.

"Did you hear anything?"

Kate thought for a moment. Then she remembered the voice and told Jake about it. "I feel I should recognize it. It was so familiar, but I just can't place it."

"Maybe you will after a while," Jake suggested.

"Maybe," Kate agreed. But how long did she have? she wondered. Did she even have a little while? That dream had left her feeling very close to death. And she didn't like the feeling. She needed to feel the heat and realness of Jake. She set the cup on the bedside table near the clock. "Come to bed with me, Jake." She pulled back the covers so he could climb in. "Hold me close, and warm me up."

Jake climbed in and took her in his arms. "How's this?"

"Wonderful," she murmured, snuggling against him and molding her body to fit the shape of his. The milk had calmed her a little, and the closeness of Jake was doing the rest. After a short while, she was finally able to go back to sleep.

Jake listened to Kate's even breathing for a long time. His mind was jumbled with fear for her, with thoughts of her dream, with wonder as to how to get past this so they could live their lives together without fear.

Jake didn't know what to do, he didn't even know how to begin to ease his fear. Since he had no real idea what the visions had been trying to tell them, he didn't know what direction to take.

One thing he did know was that he wasn't letting Kate go to teach in the morning. He wasn't letting her out of his sight again until this was over, not for anything.

Near dawn, he finally gave in to his exhaustion and allowed sleep to overtake him. He awoke some time later to the ringing of the telephone.

The clock on the table said 8:22. Jake noticed right away that Kate wasn't beside him. Her place on the bed was cold. He looked around and was touched by a cold wave of fear when he didn't hear her in the bathroom.

The telephone rang again. And to his horror, it was joined by the whistle of the smoke alarm downstairs.

He jumped out of bed, glancing quickly to make sure that she wasn't in the bathroom. He ran downstairs. She wasn't in the kitchen, which was becoming filled with smoke from a burning skillet on the stove. He moved the skillet to a cool burner, swearing loudly when its handle burned his hand. The phone rang again, and the alarm blared in his ears. He absently fanned the smoke with a towel. All the while, he tried to push down his fear for Kate, but it grew no matter how hard he tried to control it. She wasn't in the house. He swore loudly, his voice sounding hollow over the noise at the alarm and phone.

The phone rang again, and the smoke alarm finally grew quiet.

Jake grabbed the phone in the kitchen. "Hello?" he nearly growled. He turned and looked down the hall past the stairs. His heart contracted with terror. The front door was standing open.

Then the voice on the phone touched him. "May I speak with Kate McCoy, please?"

"She's not here," he said, his voice so tight with sudden fear that he could hardly speak. "I think perhaps she may have gone to work." He didn't want to face the fact that that probably wasn't true. But he still hoped. He knew, however, she wouldn't have gone without telling him, nor would she have left that skillet on the stove. He closed his eyes, trying to close out the fear he felt for her. Right then he didn't really care where she was as long as she was safe.

"Well, this is the Port James Little School, and she isn't here. We thought perhaps she was sick. Do we need to get a sub for today?"

His fear threatened to bubble over. Where the hell was she?

Jake sank into a nearby chair, his legs refusing to hold him up. "Yes," he replied, but his voice cracked with terror.

He hung up the phone and moved down the hall to the door. He stepped out onto the porch, ignoring the cool morning. He saw the newspaper, unfolded on the top step of the porch. His knees threatened to give out and he sank down on the step beside the paper, his elbows on his knees, his hands covering his face. "Oh, Kate," he moaned. "Where are you? Where the hell are you?"

CHAPTER FIFTEEN

After having such a nightmare, Kate felt like death warmed over when she woke. The gray light of dawn was forcing its way through the windows, and try as she might, she couldn't go back to sleep. Jake was sleeping deeply, snoring lightly beside her, and Kate didn't have the heart to wake him, even though she nearly gave in to the urge to kiss him. She looked at the light filtering in, and had never felt so glad to see the morning. It amazed her how much more frightening things could be in the dark.

She slipped out of bed, bringing only a soft murmur from Jake. For a long moment, she stood at the edge of the bed and watched him sleep. His strong, handsome features were relaxed. Watching him, hearing his breathing, having him in her bed, all brought about a flood of memories of the previous night. She'd never been held and touched and loved the way he'd held and touched and loved her.

Fixing his breakfast was something she wanted to do for him. She knew it didn't sound like much, compared to how he made her feel, but her heart quickened when she pictured the two of them sitting at her table, sharing breakfast in the warmth of her cozy kitchen. She slipped on her robe and fuzzy slippers and went downstairs to start breakfast. She whipped eggs in a bowl and put some butter in a skillet on the stove to melt. After glancing at the clock, she decided to call the school just as soon as she brought in the morning newspaper. After the nightmare, she had no thought of going to work. She would feel alone there, even in a room full of children. No, she wanted, she needed to stay close to Jake.

Kate stepped outside and went down the three porch steps to retrieve the newspaper. The cool morning air smelled salty. The street was empty. A dog barked somewhere on the next block, but otherwise, all was quiet.

She slid the paper out of the narrow blue plastic bag that held it and unfolded it to glance at the headline.

"Kaitlan?"

Hearing her full name sent a shiver up her spine, causing her hair to stand up on the back of her neck. She turned, thinking for the moment that she would see John, from the dreams, standing before her as though he'd come across time to throw her into the sea.

It wasn't John, however, and Kate was able to relax.

It was Mr. Taylor, calling to her from his front door. "Kaitlan, would you mind coming over here to check my toaster?" he said. "I can't seem to get the silly thing to work properly, and I'm afraid it might burn up or something."

She took a few steps down her walk toward him. "I'm not dressed, Mr. Taylor."

"Good God, Kaitlan, you're covered much more than I've seen you in the summer. And I promise this will only take a minute. By the time you get dressed, the doggone thing might catch fire and burn the whole damn house down!" he grumbled.

"Oh, all right," she finally agreed. "But I can only stay a minute. If I can't get it to work, you'll have to have something else for breakfast."

She set her newspaper on the top step of her porch and crossed the yard to him.

Mr. Taylor held open the door for her, and Kate went into his house. A slight musty smell touched her senses, and for some reason today it seemed stronger than usual. It reminded Kate briefly of her dream, but she forced the memory from her mind. Mr. Taylor's house had always had that smell, and Kate assumed it was because it never got a thorough cleaning. Mr. Taylor had a woman come every Thursday to do the laundry and clean up the kitchen and bathroom, but that was about all.

In the kitchen Kate went right to the toaster on the counter—a counter that, except for Thursday afternoons and Friday mornings after the cleaning lady visited, usually held a fine layer of dust and grease.

Two pieces of bread were sticking out of the toaster. Kate pushed down the lever and the bread disappeared. The coils inside the toaster began to glow.

"Looks to me like it's toasting," she muttered.

She looked up to find Mr. Taylor staring at her with a strange glint in his eyes. The last time he'd looked at her like that was the night she'd come with Jake and he'd yelled at him to get out.

"Mr. Taylor, is something wrong?"

His face was so still that for a moment Kate thought he'd died, that any second he would pitch forward to the floor at her feet.

But then he spoke and his face came to life again. "I have something for you, Kaitlan."

"That's really nice, Mr. Taylor," she muttered. He had in the past given her small gifts such as candy and cookies in thanks for the help she gave him, so this didn't surprise her. "But I really can't stay. Can it wait until later?"

"I'm afraid it can't," he said. He took her arm and pulled her across the kitchen.

He was walking surprisingly well this morning, she thought, but allowed him to guide her. "You have to stand right here," he said.

Kate stopped where he wanted her and waited, trying to hide her impatience. She wanted to get back to her kitchen before Jake woke up to find her gone.

"Now you have to close your eyes and hold out your hand." Mr. Taylor smiled, but Kate didn't really think the smile reached his eyes. She could see this was like a game to him, and she knew she was never going to get out of there until she played it with him.

She sighed heavily. "Oh, all right," she finally agreed. She held out one hand before closing her eyes.

Something small, cool and hard landed in her palm. Something that didn't quite feel like a round piece of butterscotch candy.

"Open your eyes now, Kaitlan, dear," he instructed. Funny how his voice didn't sound so old and raspy any longer.

Kate opened her eyes and looked down at what lay in her palm. She gasped upon seeing a ring.

A beautiful emerald ring.

The same emerald ring that Jacob Krinshaw had given to Kaitlan McGregor as an engagement ring. The same ring John Tallon had torn off Kaitlan McGregor's finger.

Fear, stark, precise and vivid, gripped her instantly. Her eyes met his in that same instant.

"Where did you get this?" It was no more than a whisper. She could barely speak. Her complete insides felt clenched in one giant knot of cold terror.

He smiled, a large, evil smile that revealed all his teeth. His bottom teeth were crooked, just as she'd feared they would be. Just as John's teeth had been in the vision she and Jake shared.

"From you, Kaitlan. On that Fourth of July so long ago."

Kate tore her gaze from his to look down at the third finger of her left hand. A small scab was still there where the finger was healing after that vision in which Jacob had been killed, and John had torn the engagement ring from Kaitlan's finger.

There was no denying that it was the same ring she now held in her hand.

Kate shook her head, refusing to believe his words, refusing to believe what was coming to light. "John Tallon?" she whispered. She forced herself to meet his glistening gaze once again and knew that John Tallon and Jonathan Taylor were the same man. "That's impossible," she whispered. Then she drew in a long breath. Fear was twisting around her lungs, making it hard to draw in any air.

"Of course it isn't," he said through that horrifying smile. "I'm sure you don't know, but I stood on that cliff all those years ago, after the sea had swallowed you both, and I watched the fireworks. I thought briefly of turning myself in, at least until I realized I'd done the right thing."

"The right thing?" she screeched at him.

"Yes," he went on calmly. "I wanted you so much, I would have killed Krinshaw a hundred times over in order to have you, although I was surprised that it had been so easy to do. Then when you rushed at me, I saw that even though he was gone, you'd still never have me, because you'd seen me kill him. And if I couldn't have you, I wasn't about to leave you for someone else. So shoving you in to follow your lover was the right thing, the only thing."

Kate blinked trying to find any logic in his words. She found none. She opened her mouth to speak, but no words would come.

"So I stood there and watched the fireworks. Then I went home. I missed you terribly. And I must admit I was very surprised when I found you again in 1931. I had just moved into this house, wanting to be close to where you grew up. And suddenly there you were. Of course, I had to kill you again. You'd have gone to the police if I hadn't."

"Oh, God," Kate croaked, wishing she didn't believe anything he was saying.

"Then again sometime in the mid-fifties—I can't remember the exact date—there you were again. You nearly escaped me then." His voice was soft, but strong and even. He could have been simply reminiscing with an old friend about an ordinary holiday in the past.

Kate was suddenly glad she hadn't eaten breakfast yet that morning. She'd be sick by now if there'd been anything at all in her stomach.

"And now, when I'm such an old man, here you are again. At first, I was going to let it go. I thought perhaps there was the chance that you wouldn't recognize me." He paused, studying her intently. "But then you brought *him* here. You actually brought Krinshaw right into my own living room. If I'd been ten years younger, I'd have jumped out of the chair and killed him right there. But I guess I'll have to bide my time now. He's so much younger than I."

Kate made a strangled sound and tried to step back. But like the rest of her body, which felt as if it had shut down with fear, her legs and feet refused to work. She knew she should move. She should run. She could easily outrun him. He was just an old man, after all. Just when she thought she was going to get her body to respond to the commands of her brain, he went on.

"Put it on for me, Kaitlan. Let me see it on your finger one last time."

When Kate didn't move, he did. He picked up the ring and slipped it onto her finger. It fit perfectly.

"I'm sorry it has to be this way, dear Kaitlan."

The sound of his voice registered in her brain. It was the voice of her dream. Oh, dear God, her mind cried out, he was going to bury her alive.

That thought got her feet moving. But she'd only taken one step when he put a wrinkled old hand on her chest and shoved her.

It wasn't a very hard shove, but it took her off guard. She stumbled away, noticing for the first time that while she'd had her eyes closed, he'd swung open the door leading to his basement. The stairs were right behind her. Kate tumbled through the doorway. She grabbed at the thin board that posed as a banister and missed it, falling backward down the stairs.

She fell into nothing more than air. And thoughts of the cliff, the rocks and the raging sea passed through her mind. She thought she was falling just as Kaitlan had fallen over the cliff. Any second, she expected to land in the icy, cold sea. A startled cry escaped her.

She missed the top half of the stairs altogether. When her feet finally touched down on the eighth step, she was only knocked farther backward. She tumbled down the remaining steps, and at the bottom, her head crashed onto the floor.

It made little difference that the floor was of earth and not the sea as she'd expected. To Kate it felt more like stone. She vaguely thought she must have landed on one of the huge rocks below the cliff. Pain shot through her head and the rest of her body in a single instant like an explosion. Darkness followed. Darkness like the cold sea finally washed over her. And then there was nothing.

Less than a block away, Jake was sitting at the kitchen table after having quickly dressed. He rested his elbows on the table and held his face in his hands, trying to decide how to find Kate. Perhaps she'd gone to pick up a gallon of milk or something.

Jake knew better. He knew that whatever had happened to the two other teachers known as Kate was now happening to Kate McCoy. He closed his eyes and concentrated on Kate. For so many days now, he'd been linked to her. He knew her feelings. He knew when she was in danger. He felt her fear. He concentrated now, trying to see her, trying to see where she might be. But he saw nothing. He felt nothing.

Did that mean she was already dead?

Hell, no. He refused to believe it. He couldn't lose her now. Not when it had taken him all his life to find her.

"Where are you, Kate?" he yelled into the empty kitchen. "Tell me where you are!" He slammed his fist against the table.

No answer came to him.

Jake had never before known such frustration. "There just has to be something in the visions and dreams. Something that I missed," he said out loud, trying to think.

Jake was concentrating on John Tallon. Tallon was the killer, and Jake was certain that Tallon had something to do with Kate's disappearance, as well as that of those other two women. But he had no idea how to go about finding the man. He rooted through Kate's kitchen drawers until he found a telephone book. But it did him little good. There wasn't one single Tallon in the entire Port James area.

But even if Tallon was still alive, he'd be a very old man, Jake thought. Perhaps he had a son, or perhaps his spirit had moved on to someone else. Jake raked his fingers through his hair and moved to look out Kate's back door. He hoped and wished to see something, *anything,* that would at least point him in Kate's direction.

He looked out into the backyard. It was dreary, still wet from the past few days of rain. The trees were bare.

His study moved across the yard. He could see the back of Mr. Taylor's yard. And what he saw brought instant memories. Memories that turned his blood cold.

He—no, Jacob Krinshaw—had gotten the rose he gave to Kaitlan from Tallon. Tallon knew flowers and plants better than anyone. Because Tallon was... Dear God, Tallon was the florist!

And Mr. Taylor's yard was filled with shrubs and perennial plants. And rosebushes. They had been cut back and covered with mulch for the winter, but Jake could see they were rosebushes. And what had Kate said—that the old man loved to work in his garden. Could Taylor be Tallon?

He knew he was taking a chance. But it was the only chance he had. He ran out the door and down Kate's driveway. He didn't stop until until he reached Taylor's front door.

Could Jonathan Taylor be Tallon? he still wondered. It's possible, his mind replied. He'd be about the right age. But he's just an old man. Yes, but Kate doesn't suspect him. That would give Taylor an advantage over her. In Jake's thoughts, questions and answers just kept popping out, like some mental debate.

The front door was open, and Jake started to knock and call out. From where he stood, he could see down the hall into the kitchen.

He saw the basement door was open. And one of Kate's fuzzy red slippers sat on the floor near it. Icy-cold fear shivered through him, and he nearly pulled the door from its hinges as he tugged it open. Inside, he bit his tongue to keep from calling out Kate's name. He didn't want to give Taylor the advantage of letting him know that Jake was in his house. He moved silently and quickly to the kitchen where he listened for several seconds, seconds that felt more like hours.

The dull sound that finally came to him was a cross between a swish and a scrape. He only needed to hear it once to recognize what it was.

Shoveling.

And it was coming from the basement. Jake moaned, ignoring the fear that rippled through him. Oh, God, he was already too late. Kate was dead, and Jonathan Taylor was burying her in the basement.

He raced down the steps just in time to see the old man toss another shovelful of earth into the hole in the basement floor. "Stop!" he cried out, hardly recognizing his own voice.

Jonathan Taylor did stop and looked up at him. It was evident he was surprised to see Jake. "You!" he said, surprised.

Jake had the impression Taylor hadn't expected him so soon. Jake took the rest of the steps to the bottom, just as Taylor came at him with the shovel held high.

Taylor, as Tallon, had been at one time Jake's height and size, but age had taken its toll. Now Jake had no problem wrestling the shovel from the old man and shoving him away. Taylor landed in a heap in the far corner of the basement. Jake moved to the hole. It was just the right size for a small adult. Just the right size for Kate, he thought with horror. He peered down and saw her hand. One still hand. An emerald ring sparkled up at him from her third finger. The rest of her was completely covered with earth.

Jake dropped the shovel and grabbed that hand. He tugged on it, bringing out her whole arm. With one hand, he shoved the earth aside while he pulled on her at the same time. He pulled until he finally had her out. He drew her small, lifeless form to him. He brushed the dirt from her face, causing her head to fall away from him limply.

"Kate, oh, Kate..." he moaned.

"It's too late. She's already dead," said Jonathan Taylor from the corner.

"Shut up, old man!" Jake snapped. He laid Kate on the cool floor and felt for a pulse. It was there, though just barely. But she wasn't breathing. He remembered how she'd revived him, and he wasn't sure he could do the same for her. He'd never had any formal first-aid training. He was about to hold her nose and blow into her mouth when he remembered what she'd said about her dream, that dirt had fallen into her mouth when she'd tried to scream.

He turned her head to the side and opened her mouth. Dirt fell out. He scooped more out with his finger, hoping it was enough. Then he filled her lungs with his own air.

With one puff, she coughed and seemed to come back to life, choking and gasping at the same time. Jake watched her, letting her cough it out herself. Besides, he felt such relief pour over him at seeing her alive. He couldn't quite move.

"Hold me," she said, her voice cracking. "Just hold me. Don't let me go." She clung to him, sobbing, her tears making streaks through the dirt on her face. Her eyes looked like large, bright, shining emeralds standing out through the dirt.

And he'd never been so glad to see her. She'd never felt so good in his arms. "Never, never, love," he said softly, feeling tears in his own eyes.

He moved finally to take her upstairs, to get her out of the musty, horrible cellar. He helped her to her feet, keeping his arms around her as tightly as possible while he led her up the stairs.

"I think you've broken my leg," Jonathan Taylor called out to them from the corner where he still remained. His voice once again sounded raspy, like an old man's.

"You're lucky it wasn't your neck!" Jake replied without looking at him.

He helped Kate into the kitchen where he sat her down on a chair. But she sat for only a moment, refusing to let him go even long enough to call the police and get her a drink of water. He had to take her with him. Not that he minded, really. He was pretty reluctant to let her go, too.

"How do you feel?" he asked, helping her hold the glass while she took a drink.

"Like my insides are shaking apart," she replied. Even her voice sounded shaky. "Like my throat is still full of dirt." She sniffed. She looked up at him, her eyes huge and round and filled with the terror she must have felt. "I was going to die, Jake," she said slowly, as though the words brought about another round of horror.

They did for Jake, but he pushed the fear aside for once. "But you didn't, and he can't hurt you anymore."

She started to cry again, and attempted to smile through her tears. "I feel like such an idiot. He lured me over here by telling me his toaster was broken."

Jake leaned down beside her and tenderly brushed dirt from her cheek with his thumb.

"How did you know where to find me?" she asked. She absently wiped away a tear; then she took his hand and held it tightly.

"His hobby gave him away." At her puzzled look, he went on. "Krinshaw bought that rose from him."

She gasped, her eyes growing even larger. "It was right there all the time, and we never saw it, never made the connection."

He gave her hand a squeeze. "What's important is that I saw it in time to save you," he said softly.

They heard a distant siren.

Officer Hewer arrived within moments, and together, Jake and Kate let him in. Explaining the situation in bits and pieces, they led him to the basement. He was followed by two more policemen and a state trooper. And within minutes, an entire team of investigators and an ambulance arrived.

Kate still held Jake's hand as she watched the paramedics take Jonathan Taylor away on a gurney after he'd been arrested. For a brief moment, his eyes met hers. Those eyes were full of such hate. And Kate recognized that look of hate. It was the same look he'd had when she stepped on his foot in that alley where he kissed her. The look made her shiver. With her free hand, she held her robe closed tightly at her throat, and watched him go.

And for the first time, even though she was cold, she felt no fear. She felt only pity. It was an empty feeling, but a welcome one after such terror.

Two hours later, they were still at Taylor's house.

Kate was standing in the musty basement, trying to ignore that moldy smell that now threatened to make her sick. It reminded her so much of the earth that she still tasted in her mouth. Jake stood behind her, his hand resting lightly on her shoulder to let her know he was there with her. She had the feeling he needed to keep touching her as much as she needed him to touch her.

They stood watching a group of investigators and forensic scientists who were digging up the earth floor.

Officer Hewer stood with them. His surprise had not yet worn off. "I still can't believe that old man was capable of such a crime," he said for what must have been the hundredth time.

Neither Kate nor Jake offered him any reply. They were too busy waiting.

"I found something," one of the diggers called out.

Everyone stopped and gathered around him. Kate held her breath. Jake's squeeze of her shoulder was a comfort, and she reached up with one hand to hold on to him. She'd known this would come, and still she dreaded hearing the words. They would make the nightmare so much more real. At least there was no longer any of that dead, cold terror. There was, however, dread. But Kate could face that. Especially with Jake so near.

"It's a bone," the digger confirmed.

"Damn! I can't believe it," muttered Hewer.

Jake brought his arms around Kate to pull her back against him. She leaned on him, welcoming the strength she felt in his arms. So many emotions were swirling around her in at that moment that she felt her knees might buckle beneath her. Joy that the ordeal was over and the fear was gone. Sadness that all she and Jake had experienced in the visions was true, and four people had lost their lives needlessly. Anxiety that there could be more for the investigators to find, more than even she and Jake knew.

"Human?" someone asked.

"Looks to be. It'll have to be tested before I can say for sure."

At hearing those words, Kate felt a tear slide down her cheek again. She didn't wipe it away or try to hide it. Those two missing teachers and Jacob Krinshaw and Kaitlan McGregor had lost so much. And all because of one man's obsession. They deserved her tears. They deserved to have someone finally feel for them after so many years.

Jake leaned up close to Kate. "Come on, honey," he said softly. "Let's go home. We've seen what we needed to see."

They left quietly, still holding hands. And for the first time in days, Kate didn't feel cold.

EPILOGUE

Jake watched Kate from a distance.

It was nearly two weeks since Kate's brush with death. And a lot had happened since.

For starters, there'd been no more dreams. Jake wasn't sure whether he was glad or not. The dreams and visions had somehow held them together.

He'd gone back to Willows Point to finish the carousel and left Kate to her teaching. And he'd missed her more than he'd ever have thought possible. He hoped Kate felt the same way. Since there were no more dreams, he could no longer feel what she was feeling.

True, he wanted her. And he wanted her to want him. But he had to face the fact that he was no longer linked to her as he had been.

So now he just watched her.

Michael Krinshaw had had memorials erected for both Kaitlan McGregor and Jacob Krinshaw, and Kate had just finished putting flowers on them. Roses, Jake saw. Red roses for both of them.

She turned and saw him, and a smile lit up her face.

That's a good sign, he thought. At least she was glad to see him. But did she want him as desperately as he wanted her?

He had no choice but to find out. The waiting and wondering was killing him.

He walked toward her and took both her hands in his.

"Hi," she said, looking up at him.

"Hi."

"I missed you. You left without hardly saying a word."

He felt like a heel, knowing she told the truth, but he hadn't felt ready to talk about anything. He hadn't felt ready to say what he thought needed to be said. And he wasn't sure Kate was ready even yet to hear what he had to say.

"I know. I'm sorry." He didn't know what else to say. With Kate, he'd known such fear. But it had never been fear of Kate. It had always been fear *for* Kate. This was a new fear. It was a fear of her wanting to walk out of his life.

She turned slightly and looked down at the memorials. "Do you think it was their spirits guiding us? Or do you think people in different times really live right beside us in other dimensions?"

Jake hadn't given it much thought at all. He'd been too busy thinking of Kate.

"Come on, Jake. Tell me what you think," she persisted, looking back at him. Her green eyes twinkled.

He glanced at the memorials, then met her gaze. "What do I think?" he echoed. "I think their love was just too strong to die, even when they did. I think it might have even searched until it found us. And I think it brought us together because we were meant to be."

"So you think finding their killer was just an added little bonus?" she questioned.

Jake let go of one of her hands so they could walk, and they turned away from the memorials. They walked slowly through the cool dampness of the day, toward their cars. "No," he said finally. "I think finding the killer was most important. If we hadn't, there was the chance of the love dying if Taylor killed you." It sounded like a simple enough explanation, and Jake wasn't even sure if he believed it. What he did believe was that he loved Kate and there was no way he could let that love die. Not now. Not ever.

"I suppose it really doesn't matter, does it? The why, I mean. But it is important that they be at peace," she said, taking a deep breath of clean, crisp, salty air. She glanced back at the memorials. "I don't think I'll ever get tired of feeling clean air in my lungs," she added.

"I'm sure," Jake said, studying her, wondering again just what she was thinking.

"So it's all over, isn't it? I haven't had a dream that I remember in the past week."

"Not all of it," replied Jake.

Kate stopped walking, her surprise at his reply evident. "It's not?"

"Of course it's not. Kaitlan and Jacob never married. And they were supposed to," he stated rather bluntly.

"But they're dead," Kate put in.

"We're not."

Kate could only stare at him.

Jake gave her hand a squeeze and started walking. They reached her car.

"I know it's happening pretty fast. But it feels so right," he went on. "We'll have to slow it down a little, I think, at least while I finish the carousel and you finish out the year of teaching."

They stood at her car, and Kate looked up at him, her eyes huge with anticipation.

"But I'm willing to give it a try. We could take it slow," he continued. "Spend the weekends together. You wouldn't have to actually think about getting married until the summer."

Kate stared at him again. "Married?"

"Will you at least say you'll think about it?" he asked. The fact that she wasn't saying much of anything was scaring him, almost as much as he had been scared when he thought he'd lost her.

"I don't have to think about it," she said finally. "I'll marry you."

"You will?"

"Yes."

"When?"

"Is the Fourth of July too far away?"

Jake smiled. "I'll try to wait that long."

Kate held up her hand and looked down at the emerald ring that was still on her finger. "I nearly gave this to Michael, but for some strange reason, I really didn't want to take it off. What do you think I should do with it?"

"Keep it," he said. "It's always been yours."

* * * * *

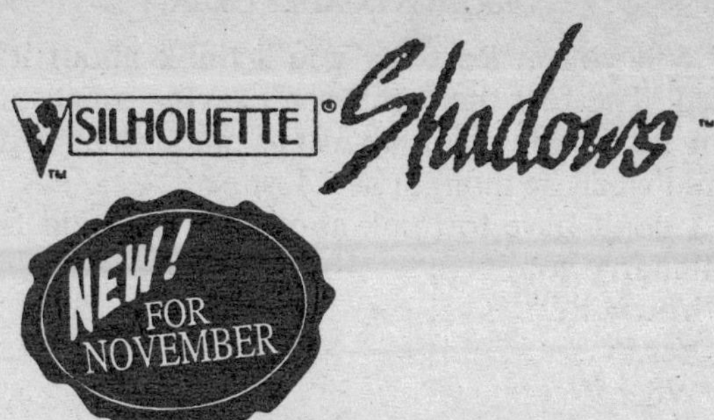
SILHOUETTE
Shadows
NEW!
FOR
NOVEMBER